KEEPERS OF MAGIC

THE PSYCHE TREE: BOOK ONE

BY DAVID CAINE

Uncle Steve,

I hope you enjoy reading my book, and remember, there's always magic inside of you!

David Caine

DORRANCE
PUBLISHING CO
EST. 1920
PITTSBURGH, PENNSYLVANIA 15238

The contents of this work, including, but not limited to, the accuracy of events, people, and places depicted; opinions expressed; permission to use previously published materials included; and any advice given or actions advocated are solely the responsibility of the author, who assumes all liability for said work and indemnifies the publisher against any claims stemming from publication of the work.

Dorrance Publishing Co
585 Alpha Drive
Pittsburgh, PA 15238
Visit our website at *www.dorrancebookstore.com*

ISBN: 978-1-6853-7429-7
eISBN: 978-1-6853-7573-7

KEEPERS OF MAGIC

THE PSYCHE TREE: BOOK ONE

For my Zayda,

Who always taught me to draw on the walls,

And write from my heart

Thank you for inspiring me everyday,

and I hope this inspires you to share your writing as well

Prologue

OGER CRASHED THROUGH THE LEAFY BUSHES OF THE SCHOOL'S lush forest, huffing and puffing, nearly out of breath, but he couldn't stop. Branches whipped across his face, splintering him in multiple places. He looked behind him, trying to find the creature that was chasing him, but the darkness of the night and density of the trees prevented him from seeing much. Suddenly, he felt his shoe get caught on something on the ground, and he tripped, splattering his face with mud. Some of it even got into his mouth. He turned around to see a thick branch had been lying on the ground, sticking up just enough to trip him.

He quickly got back up, and started sprinting, rubbing his hands on his pants and spitting mud onto the ground. "Help!" he cried out, but to no avail. Nobody would hear him out here, this late at night. What was he thinking, sneaking out in the middle of the night? Roger had been going to Mrs. Hearther's School of the Sciences for two years now, since he was eighteen. He had chosen zoology to study, he had made many friends over the past two years, and had certainly never broken a single rule before. He was a model student! So why suddenly did he now decide that it was time to do just that? Why decide to sneak out past curfew?

The answer: He didn't know. Something had compelled him to keep moving, like his mind had been taken over. It was like somebody was in his body, forcing him to go to that building. The only person who would be able to do that would be a psychologist, but none of them were that evil. Right? He tried to fight it off, but he couldn't; it was too strong. It was a type of magic he had never felt before. His instructors had never taught him how to defend himself if something controlled his mind! They had never even mentioned anything like this before in his foreign species class, or in his magical beings lessons. What did this person want from him? He was just a regular zoologist, just like everybody else.

He tried to use what his instructors had taught him and used his mind link to call to the animals, the squirrels, the wild horses, foxes, crows, cicadas, anything that would listen, but he couldn't. Whatever was controlling him didn't want him to use his powers to escape. Either that, or this person took it away from him. But that also wasn't possible. Was it? Could you really take away somebody's magic? Finally, after what seemed like a millennium of running, he broke free of the forest and was out in the open of the school's vast field. He tried to call for help again, but as soon as he opened his mouth to scream, nothing came out. A sharp burn ran across his throat, preventing him from making any noise. When he tried again, the pain was stronger, and this time, it reached his head, giving him a splitting headache.

This person took something else away from him, his voice! First his ability to move freely, then his magic, and now his ability to speak. What was next? As he rounded the hill toward the back of the school, he could see the twenty-year-olds' building come into view. Somebody had to still be awake to see him running around like a madman and ask what was happening, but nobody did. He kept trying to break free, but still, he couldn't. He was in so much trouble. At least he could still think for himself.

This was it for him. They were going to find him and kick him out for leaving the building after curfew. He was going to lose everything: his magic, his friends, and his family would surely shun him out, even more than they already did. And what could he say for himself? That he just felt "compelled" to break the rules. That he couldn't fight the urge to run toward the building? Nobody would believe him!

He tried to formulate a plan, but the sight of the building getting closer and closer was clouding his thoughts, stressing him out even more than he already was. Suddenly, a couple of yards away from the front doors of the building, he felt his body being tugged to the left, away from the building. He tried to stay out in the open, so if somebody was out, they would see him. But whatever was controlling him forced him to slowly creep on the edge of the building, close to the shadows. The slow walking dragged on the process, only making him more terrified for his life. But while he was petrified for his life, a little bit of confusion swept through Roger's mind. Why did this person do that? Why turn left? There was nothing out there. The only thing this far back was more field and the...oh.

There was literally nothing out there. There was a mysterious cliff out the back of the school that all of the instructors told the students not to go near. Nobody knew what it led to, if anything. It was just a giant crack in the ground spreading for miles in every direction. An unexplainable thick fog coated the inside the void, preventing people from seeing further down than about fifty yards. It could just stop there, it could go on for a vast amount of miles, or it could never end. Nobody knew and nobody wanted to know.

Nobody in the school's history had ever gone near the cliff. He was really going to die. The thing was, he didn't understand why. Why was this thing doing this to him? He had never done anything wrong in his life. Why him? He was trying to come up with answers as to why this was happening to him, when suddenly, it was as if his brain shut off. It was like the lightbulb just flicked off leaving an empty void, ready for invasion. He couldn't think for himself.

"You little peasant," whispered a voice in his head. It was a wispy dream-like voice, not loud, but not quiet. It wasn't masculine or feminine. It wasn't human or animal. Somehow, it was all of those combined. It was as if there were thousands of voices speaking to him through his head, all at the same time, delivering the same message. "It was nothing that you did. Now, this is the cliche part where the bad guy tells the good guy their whole plan, but the good guy gets away and tells everybody, foiling the bad guy's plan and saving the day. Well, that's not going to happen. See, we calculated every move, everything that would happen to get you to this moment. And I won't have the slight chance of you living through this ruining our plans."

All Roger could do was watch. He couldn't do anything, say anything, think anything. All he could do was watch as this thing slowly brought him toward the cliff. Somehow, he was able to shut his eyes. The fear of not wanting to watch as his body tumble like a limp doll down the abyss was stronger than this thing's ability. Suddenly, the thing stopped. His eyes were forced open and he wished they hadn't. The abyss was, well, an abyss, but he hadn't expected it to look so menacing. Suddenly, he felt a stinging, stretching sensation all throughout his body. The pain was unbearable, but once again, he couldn't do anything about it, not even let out a scream. He suffered in silence. After a few seconds, the pain died down, and suddenly, feeling in his body returned. He could think, talk, and move again. He looked up, and what he saw startled him. It was him! Roger looked down at his hands. They looked normal, except for one key detail—they were a hazy version of their regular selves. He moved his hands to his sides so he could see his entire body, and just like his hands, they were exactly the same. What had this thing done to him? What was this image of himself staring back at him?

"Hello Roger," the other him said. It sounded like him too! Suddenly, Roger knew what was happening. When this thing had taken over his body, his voice, and his thoughts, it was copying it. It had created another him. It was going to push him down the cliff, and take his place at school. Not if he had anything to do with it.

He opened his mind to call out to the animals of the forest, but when he tried a stinging sensation coursed through his mind, starting at his temple and running down his nerves, finally reaching his feet. He crumpled down to the ground, shock in his eyes. Why couldn't he use his magic?

"What did you do to me?" Roger asked, shaking, writhing on the ground.

"Really, you need to keep up Roger," it said, playfully. "We can't have you ruining our plans. So I just took your magic away." It laughed, seemingly enjoying Roger's suffering. Roger tried to stand up, and after a few seconds of trial and error, he finally limped to his feet, favoring his right foot. He did his best to run toward the other him, ready to throw a punch, but it came out as a strut and a gentle swing. The other Roger was able to easily maneuver out of the way. Swiftly, the monster moved behind Roger and kicked him to the ground with ease.

"Looks like we have a fighter," it laughed, walking around to the front of him. The thing leaned down until it was eye level with Roger and gave him a giant, white, toothy grin. "Night, night." The thing stood up, and without another word, kicked a defeated Roger into the void, never to be seen again. A little chuckle came out of its mouth as it turned around. It walked back toward the direction of the school, preparing itself for its first day of school.

CHAPTER ONE

"GOTCHA!" YELLED TINNA, PINNING ME TO THE WET AFTERNOON GRASS. "Oh no!" I replied, falling to the ground, pretending to be hurt. "That's your third point! You won!"

"Yay!" Tinna shouted, helping me up. She wasn't strong enough to lift me yet, but she didn't have to know that. I pulled myself up, pretending to need the help of my little sister.

"Thanks. Let's head inside now," I told her, reaching my hand down to ruffle her short, brown curly hair. "It's getting late, and it's Friday night. You know what that means."

"Family dinner night!" Tinna exclaimed, bubbling with excitement. Every Friday night, both of our parents cleared their schedules so that we could have dinner as a family. It was the day Tinna and I looked forward to the most. It was the only time that our entire family was in the same room at the same time, with no distractions. We bounded across our vast expanse of a yard, splashing mud on our pants and getting blades of grass stuck in the crevices of our shoes. We raced across the well-maintained grass, and to our mansion. When we arrived at the front door, we knocked on it, and almost immediately, Mr. Daniel opened it up, revealing the grandeur of the interior.

"Good evening Miss Tinna and Master Jeremy," Mr. Daniel greeted us.

"I told you, Mr. Daniel, you don't have to call us that," I said, taking off my shoes and leaving them at the door, ready to be cleaned.

"Nonsense. Your father requires it," he replied. No matter how many times I told him, our father insisted that Mr. Daniel call us that. Once our shoes were in a neat row at the door, we used our socks to slide across the wood flooring, and into the kitchen. Before we could even arrive in the kitchen, we could already smell the food cooking. Dad was at the stove, stirring something delicious smelling. Mom was setting the table, meticulously placing the silverware, plates, and glasses.

"Daddy!" screamed Tinna, running toward her father.

"Hey Tinna," replied Dad, looking away from his cooking, reaching his arms out and scooping her up.

"What are you making?" she asked, leaning over to look at the contents of the pot. He pulled her back, not wanting her to lean too far over and fall down, onto the hot stove top.

"Not much, just a new recipe I'm trying," he said simply, putting her down on the floor, before resuming the stirring. "I call it, fish and chips."

"Hey Jeremy," said our mother, after placing the last fork on the table. "Why don't you two get cleaned up before dinner? It should be ready soon."

"Okay," we replied at the same time, dashing up the stairs to our bathrooms. I turned on the hot water and let it wash over me. After a few minutes, I turned the water off, dried myself off, and put on some new clothes.

A few minutes later, Tinna and I bounded down the stairs and ran toward the kitchen table. Dinner was now done, and it smelled even better now.

"Alright kids, let's say grace," said Dad. "Jeremy, would you like to lead us tonight?" I beamed as I recited the words we say every night.

"Bless, O Father, Thy gifts to our use and us to Thy service; for Christ's sake. Amen."

"Amen," we all said together and then started eating. It was perfect. Dad doesn't talk about anything with the Church and Mom doesn't talk about her work at the library. It was perfect! I looked around the table, Mom and Dad laughing as Tinna told them a joke. This is how it should always be. We were about halfway into our meal when we heard a knock on our door.

"I will get it," said Mr. Daniel, already heading there. I heard the door open, and Mr. Daniel greeted the stranger. After a few seconds, he came back into the dining hall. "It is for you, Master Conner," he said, motioning to my dad. Dad got up to get the door. He disappeared around the corner, going to see who the mysterious visitor was.

"Can this wait, Thomas?" I heard Dad ask.

"I'm afraid not Pastor Tursoil," replied the person at the door. "There has been a problem at the church." I couldn't hear anything else more than hushed whispers.

"Okay, I will be right there," I heard Dad say. He closed the door and then came into the room. "There has been a mix-up at the church. I have to go," he said, going for his coat.

"But what about family dinner night?" Tinna asked, whimpering.

"I'm afraid I can't stay. Sorry," replied our father. He walked across the table to stand next to Mom, and whispered something in her ear. Her eyes widened for a second, and then they went back to normal.

"What? What happened?" I asked, but Dad was already out the door.

"It is nothing," Mom replied, trying to reassure us. "Dad just needs to take care of something at the Church. He shouldn't be too long." We ate the rest of our meal in silence, and I spent most of it just picking at my food. Why couldn't he stay? Didn't he know that there was more to life than the church? That he had a family to take care of? That he had a wife to love? The church was his whole life when it should just be a part of it. I didn't know why I got my hopes up. Every family dinner night had been perfect, with no distractions, just the four of us. Didn't Dad know how important Friday nights were?

I wanted more than this. I wanted more than just occasionally passing my mother on the staircase, or Church being the longest period of time I see Dad. I wanted to go out and explore the world. Why couldn't my life be like Roger's? He got to go to Mrs. Hearther's School of the Sciences. He got to go out into the world and make a difference. He was a prodigy in zoology! He had actual friends to hang out with, to cheer him up when he was sad, and to laugh with when things were good. Tinna was the closest thing that I had to a friend. But if I went out into the world, I would leave her alone with Mom and Dad and I couldn't do that. Plus, even if I got an invitation to Mrs. Hearther's School of the Sciences, which was highly unlikely, I doubt Mom and Dad would let me go. They would just say that I'm too young, and they only let Roger go after a lot, and I mean a lot, of convincing, and because he was eighteen.

They would say that I wouldn't make any friends because I was different. So what if my skin was paler than everybody else's, like the color of milk, and my eyes the same blue as the sea. Everything else was the same, I was tall, which my parents said was a good trait, I had dark brown hair, just like my dad, but what my tutors had always made sure I knew was that I had a great personality. That I could be friends with anybody I wanted to, no matter which class they are from. They said that that was the thing that mattered the most, that I respect everybody around me, no matter how poor they looked. You never know what situation they are in.

I had always told them that that sounded cheesy, and that it wasn't true. I'm still not sure if it is true. If you were to look at somebody on the side of the road, and see them in bedraggled clothes, you don't think the first impression you would have of them is that they are poor, part of the lower class. I rarely went to the market with my parents, but when I did go, I saw all kinds of people, fat people, with their vests bulging out of their belly. I saw skinny people with no clothes, exposing their bony bodies. I knew I shouldn't judge them just as simple as that, but is it really that easy not to?

I would have to show Mom and Dad that I could do it, that I could make friends, even if I've never had any social interactions with anybody but the people from the church and the market. And so what if they were from a lower class? I could do it.

But why was I even thinking about this? I couldn't leave Tinna alone. She would be miserable. And I never want her to feel miserable. Unlike Mom and Dad, I cared about her. I had to stay here to be with her. She needed me.

When we were done with dinner, I brought the dishes to the sink, cleaned them, and then headed up to my room to go to bed. When I was brushing my teeth, I heard another knock at the door. That was strange. We had never gotten more than one visitor this late at night before. I heard Mom open the door and greet somebody. I crept downstairs and eavesdropped on their conversation and heard Mom ask them why they were here at this hour. I observed Mom talking to somebody at the door, but I didn't know who it was. The person at the door handed something to Mom, and she gasped. She looked up at the person at the door, and they nodded their head. The person then turned around and walked across the lawn, back to wherever they came from. Mom closed the door and once again, looked at the thing that was given to her.

"Jeremy! Could you come downstairs?" she called.

"Coming!" I yelled. I made an effort to stomp on the stairs, making it seem I was bounding down them. Mom gave me the envelope, and as I read who it was from, I had the same reaction as my mom. It was from Mrs. Hearther's School of the Sciences! I opened it up gingerly, trying to keep it as intact as possible. I pulled out the letter from inside. There was writing on the front side, written in dark, ominous black ink. It read:

Dear Jeremy,

Congratulations! Out of the hundreds of people in Tarenburg, you, along with twenty-four others have been selected to attend our wonderful school, that is, if you wish. Mrs. Hearther's School of the Sciences in Tarenburg is an amazing place for you to study the sciences of our world and help make it a better place! If you would like to attend, included is a one-way train ticket to our school. Once you arrive, you will be greeted as you leave the train and shown around. If you would like to attend, the train leaves on Sunday, at nine A.M. sharp. We would love for you to be a part of making this world a better, safer place.

Regards,
Mrs. Hearther

The signature was written in a different font, more wavy and fancy, and in a different ink, a shiny gold. I flipped the card over, and on its back was a symbol. It was a green circle with gold lettering around the edge, reading "Mrs. Hearther's School of the Sciences." In the center, there was a five-sided star, with smaller, minimalistic symbols on the edge of each tip: an eye, a smaller star, a sapling, a chicken, and a wrench. This must be their symbol. But what did the characters represent? I put the card back in the envelope and noticed a train ticket, just like the letter said. I took a deep breath. It's almost as if my wishful thinking earlier magically sent the letter to our door. What was I supposed to do?

CHAPTER TWO

MOST OF THE NIGHT, I TOSSED AND TURNED IN BED, THINKING about the letter I received. I had never even thought about having a career in science. And why did they choose me? What made me so special? Was it because I looked different? Was it because I was upper-class? Was it because my brother was going there? I didn't know. For most of my life, I had wanted more, to get out and help the world to be better. Now, the opportunity showed up on a silver platter, and I wasn't even sure if I wanted to take it! But this shouldn't even be a question. I couldn't leave. I had to take care of Tinna. Since Mom and Dad didn't take care of her, and Mom and Dad haven't hired a proper babysitter, she was my responsibility. After what seemed like forever, I finally fell asleep.

I woke up to the sound of somebody shuffling down the stairs. I groggily got out of bed, slipped into my slippers, and went out to see who it was. Dad was running down the stairs, looking like he was in a hurry.

"Good morning Dad!" I called down to him.

"Good morning Jeremy," he replied, without even looking at me. "I have to get to work. There is some important business I have to take care of."

"Does this have anything to do with last night?" I asked him, curious. Is whatever it was really that important?

"It is none of your business," he replied, dismissing me. I wanted to tell him about the letter, but before I could say anything, the door slammed behind him, leaving an empty foyer. Just like that, dad was back to his normal self, leaving behind the fun and freedom of Friday night. I went to the window to see if I could see which direction he was going, but when I got there, he was gone. There aren't even any footprints in the wet grass. I opened the front door to see if maybe I just couldn't see him from the window, but still, he wasn't anywhere to be seen. I decided to take a walk around to the back of the house to see if he was there, but once again, he was gone. It's like he just vanished. I walked back to the front door, grass squelching under my feet, and headed back up to my room, now having something to think about for the rest of the day.

I was playing in the living room with Tinna when Dad came home. I wanted to tell him about the letter and ask for his advice, but he went right to his study, not even taking the time to greet any of us. I didn't understand him. The train left in one day, and I still haven't had any time to talk it over with my parents, or Tinna.

"Hey Tinna, do you want to take a break really quickly? I want to go ask Mom something really quickly," I asked.

"Sure," she replied, going to the kitchen, presumably to go get a snack to eat. I got up as well, and headed to Mom's door to see if I could talk to her. As expected, the door to the library was closed. I knocked on it three times.

"Who is it?" Mom called, sounding annoyed that somebody interrupted her reading. It sounded like she was back to her normal, cold self as well.

"Mom! It's me. Can I talk to you about last night?" I asked.

"I'm sorry sweety, I can't. Go ask your father," she replied, dismissively. "But do you really want to go to that school? You never had any interest in science and you have everything that you need here. Plus you won't even make any friends. You seriously want to go there?"

"What? But...Mom...how could you? Why would you... you know what, okay, fine," I sighed. How could she say that? I wanted to scream back at her about how she and Dad were terrible at raising us. God, I wanted to scream so bad. But that wouldn't get me anywhere. I knew she wouldn't understand. None of them did. They didn't know me.

"Why don't you just go? You don't need their permission," said a voice behind me. I turned around and was surprised to see who it was. "It's okay if you want to go," said Tinna.

"Go where?" I asked quickly, maybe too quickly. Did she know about the letter? But how? None of us had told her yet. I tried to act like I wasn't furious with Mom and Dad. Had to act like everything was fine for Tinna, right?

"Mrs. Hearther's School of the Sciences, silly. Where else would you go?" I guess she does know. There was no hiding it now.

"How did you know about it? Nobody told you yet," I asked.

"Please, do you seriously think I don't have ears? I heard you and Mom at the door last night, so I snuck out of my room to listen into what was going on. Then, later last night, I snuck into your room to read the letter."

"What! You sneaky little devil," I said, laughing, trying to forget what Mom had said.

"I know," she replied, with a big grin on her face, looking smug. "By the way, you are a very loud sleeper," she said.

"I am not!" I replied, defending myself. I got back on topic.

"But I would be leaving you," I replied sadly, "I couldn't do that. You're only eight years old. Mom and Dad don't look out for us. Who would take care of you?"

"I can take care of myself," she replied confidently. "And if I need help, I always have Mr. Daniel. I have seen you make meals before and I always have my dolls and cars to play with."

"But won't you be lonely without anybody to talk to?" I asked.

"If this is your dream, and I see that it is, then you should do it. You shouldn't have Mom and Dad dictate everything that happens in your life. You're sixteen now! You can make your own choices."

"Who are you, and what did you do with Tinna Tursoil?" I asked jokingly.

"I'm right here!" she replied. I wanted to keep arguing with her, that she would be lonely without me, and that she needs me. But I also know that she was right. She always had Mr. Daniel, and if it was my dream, I should take it, wherever it may lead me.

"You know, for only being eight, you still give really good advice. Are you sure you will be okay?" I asked. I was grateful that she was doing this for me, but I didn't want her to feel lonely while I was gone.

"I'll be fine!" she exclaimed, probably annoyed that I was still talking about this.

"Thank you," I told her.

"You're welcome. But you owe me when you get back."

"Alright," I replied, "Now head up to your room. I need to pack." As she went up the stairs, I wondered, what do I pack? The letter hadn't said anything about that. Well, I should probably bring a few pairs of clothes, some for night-time, some for the day, my toothbrush, and the train ticket. I packed all of that along with a few mementos of home into a duffel bag and put it by the door so it was ready for me in the morning.

Once again, I couldn't sleep. There was too much on my mind. This was the first time I had ever done something that Mom and Dad would dis-approve of. But once they see how much I would have learned in my first year, they would surely let me go back for the rest of the four years. Right? I lay awake in bed, staring up at the ceiling, until finally, sleep came to me, and I drifted off.

"Jeremy! Wake up!" My mother called, leaning into my door. "Get ready for Church!" I jolted up. I had completely forgotten. How could I forget? It was Sunday! We had to go to Church! I checked my watch; it said 6:30 A.M. I had to get ready! What was I going to tell Mom and Dad? I would have to make something up then and there if they caught me. I rushed to get ready, grabbed my bag, and headed downstairs. I opened the front door and was about to make a run for it, when Mom stopped me.

"Where do you think you are going?" she asked me.

"I—uh—wanted to go to church early?" I answered. That sounded too much like a question. Would she see through me? Wow, I couldn't think of anything else? I am so busted.

"Hmm," she replied, seemingly thinking it over. "Well good for you. But why aren't you wearing church clothes? And what is in that bag?" she asked, pointing to the duffel bag with the stuff I would bring to Mrs. Hearther's.

"Oh, this? My church clothes are in here?" I replied, slowly. "Yeah! I didn't want to get them messed up before I got there." That sounded believable, right?

"Okay," she replied, after a few seconds. "But make sure you eat something before you go."

"Okay!" I replied, maybe too loudly. "I will just have some toast on my way there." I went to the kitchen, where I saw Dad and Tinna eating. Dad was too into the morning paper to realize that I was there. Tinna looked up and I winked at her.

"Miss you," I whispered to her.

"Miss you more," she whispered back. I said goodbye to Dad, and he just gave me a little wave in return. As I said goodbye to Mom, I passed Mr. Daniel walking down the stairs.

"Good luck," he said as he saw me. I turned around, confused about why he said that. He gave me a little wink, as if knowing that I was going to Mrs. Hearther's. I smiled back, and mouth the words "thank you." I closed the front door behind me and then was out in the morning air. I check my watch: 7:15. Perfect! I had plenty of time to get to the train station before the train left. I walked toward the direction of the train station, and I got there in less than an hour.

I entered the building and showed the ticketmaster my ticket. He was too busy stamping my ticket to realize that I was just a kid without any parents around. He gave me back my ticket, and I went to find the correct track. Once I did, I found a bench and waited. I stared at the wall, thinking about if I made the right choice. I did. I wanted this. I just have to figure out which science I want to study. The school studied five main sciences: Botany, Zoology, Astronomy, Engineering, and Psychology. I didn't know which one I wanted to study yet, but I would have a lot of time to think about it on the train ride. But one thing was for certain: I would be able to see Roger again, after two years.

"Now boarding: Train to Mrs. Hearther's School of the Sciences," stated the intercom system. I hopped up, out of my seat, and waited for the train to come to a stop. Once it did, I hopped on along with a couple more kids, and then the doors shut. This was it. This was where my entire life changed, either for the better, or worse. I sighed, thinking about Tinna, how lonely she would be. No, she said that she would be alright. The train started moving, screeching along the track. Well, there was no going back now.

CHAPTER THREE

A S SOON AS THE DOORS SHUT, EVERYBODY STARTED MOVING AT once, like cattle that were just released from their pens. All of the kids dispersed into different rooms, leaving me alone with my thoughts. What if I didn't make any friends? What if this was all a mistake? I didn't even know what class I wanted to take. I should just take one step at a time. The first thing I needed to do was find somewhere to sit.

Taking a deep breath, I started walking toward the different rooms, peeking in to see which one looked best. The first one was full, with two boys and two girls, so I couldn't go in there. The second one had two people in there, about my age. I could go in there, but they were blasting music from their radio, flicking on and off the lights, and I think I saw an illegal drink or two being exchanged between them. I didn't think those were the kind of people I wanted to be friends with. I walked past them, trying to ignore what I had just seen. If I reported them, I was going to look like the bad guy to every kid here, just waiting for somebody to do something wrong, so I could tell the teachers, and get them to like me. I arrived at the third door, put my face against the glass, and saw two kids, a boy and a girl.

The boy was keeping to himself, writing in his journal, and fidgeting with his mud-stained fingers. He was wearing long pants with a few holes in them. On one of his shoes, the sole was tearing away from the actual shoe. He was tall, having to hunch over to not hit his head on the cabinets above the seats. He had long black hair that covered his eyes.

The girl was walking around the room, pacing back and forth, as if waiting for something. She was almost as tall as me, with curly brown hair and black eyes. She wore a casual skirt with a tucked-in long sleeve shirt that was stained in multiple places. Were these the kind of people I wanted to hang out with? The kind of people that looked like they just got picked up from the side of the road? They looked like they just got back from working a day in the fields. I didn't want to hang out with people of a lower class.

I started to walk to the next room, when I stopped and remembered what my tutors always told me—I shouldn't judge people by the way they looked. But by the way they looked, it seemed like they would mug me! I mean, they would probably do anything just to have decent looking clothes. But the words of my tutors interrupted my thoughts again. Ughh, it was only a few hours and the real world was already more complicated than my life at home.

"Hey, you!" a voice called from behind me. I turned around and saw a man, probably in his thirties with a bright red suit and a red hat to match it. His suit was outlined with gold lining.

"Me?" I asked, pointing to myself.

"No, not you, the person behind you, yes you! Find a seat!"

"Alright, sorry," I said, looking around me. The other rooms all looked full. I would have to go into the room with the boy and the girl. I started making my way back, the man's eyes following me the entire way. I slid the door open and as I walked inside, both kids looked up. I closed the door behind me as the boy greeted me with a little nod. I looked back at the man, and he gestured to me with his eyes. I sighed and closed the door behind me. As soon as I did, the girl ran over to me and gave me a hug!

"Hi! My name is Amanda! Isn't this great! I can't believe I was asked to go. I have always been interested in astronomy. And now, I can become a master in it! What's your name? What do you want to study? And why do you look different?"

"Uh, well," I replied, not sure of myself. Do I really tell this stranger who I was? What would I tell her? Well, I suppose if I wanted to make friends, I would have to start somewhere. "My name is Jeremy. Jeremy Tursoil." I started to tell them more, but they both looked as if they were taken aback by what I said. Even the boy perked his head up and put his pen down. Was it something I said?

"Oh. Well, I guess you might want to find another room then. You probably wouldn't want to hang out with us. I'm sorry," Amanda said. She gave me a little bow and opened the door for me.

"Why do you want me to leave?" I asked, confused. I mean, I wouldn't mind trying to find another room, but the man was probably still out there. I figured I might as well give this a try if I wanted to make any friends at all. "We were just getting to know each other," I tried.

"Sir, I don't believe that you would like to be around people of the middle- and lower class," said the boy. And just as he said that, a lightbulb turned on in my head, and the gears started turning. I understood now. Since they were middle- and lower-class citizens, they were taught to respect the upper-class people. In this case, that was me. But they seemed like nice people, and those man's eyes looking straight into my soul were still stuck in my mind. No way I would be leaving this car. I might as well keep trying.

"That doesn't mean anything. And how did you know that I was upper-class? Did I say something?" I asked them.

"Well, you said your name was Jeremy Tursoil. Only upper-class citizens have last names. And I recognized that last name. Your father is the pastor of the church. You're one the wealthiest people on this bus aside from the Mallery twins. They're in the second room, partying up a storm. The only reason that they're in is because their father is a scientist, so he bought their way in. You know, they used to be really nice. I only got to talk to them once, but during that one interaction, they seemed like perfectly normal kids. That is, until their mom passed away. That was a couple of years ago. Ever since then, they have just fallen apart. Their grades dropped, they started drinking, and their father didn't do anything about it." Amanda's eyes started to drift, like she was remembering a better time, but then they snapped back to normal. "But if you want to hang out with them, that is perfectly okay with us, right?" she asked the boy.

"Yes. We wouldn't want you to feel out of place, sir," the boy replied. But something inside me told me not to leave. These people seemed interesting and before they knew that I was upper-class, they actually wanted to talk to me. They wanted to be my friend.

"Well just because I am upper-class, doesn't change the fact that I want to get to know you. If the Mallery twins are like you say they are, and I already saw what they are doing, I don't want to be around them. My whole life, I have wanted to have more, but not in the way that you think. While I was growing up, I could have anything that I wanted, just as long as I asked. Everything was just handed to me. I don't want my life to be like that anymore. I want to go out and help Tarenburg be a better place."

"Well you don't sound like any upper-class citizen I have met, but then again, I haven't met many. I'm from the middle class. It's rare for middle-class citizens to go to Mrs. Hearther's School of the Sciences, but here I am. I'm sorry we judged you. It's just that for our whole lives we have been judged, just because we are from a lower class. Also, we didn't let you finish answering my questions. Sorry," Amanda said, apologetically. "I'm actually surprised you haven't heard of the twins. You know, being upper class and everything."

"I haven't been around many people before. My parents keep me holed up in our house twenty-four seven. They say it's because I look different, so nobody would like me, but I don't know. I don't really know how this happened. I was born this way. Do you not like me because I look different?" I asked them.

"No, why would you say that? Trust me, we know what it is like to be different, to be shunned by everybody else. We have that in common, Jeremy. All of us are judged wrongly because of the way we look and the way that we treat life. But just as a warning, not everybody in the school will be as accepting as we are," Amanda replied.

"I will keep that in mind," I replied. "And about your other question, I'm not sure what I want to study. What about you?" I asked the boy. "What's your name? What do you want to study?" He looked up toward Amanda, as if for confirmation that he could talk to me. Amanda nodded.

"My name is Rohan," he said finally. "My family and I are from the lower class. Lower-class citizens don't get to go to schools like Mrs. Hearther's, but somebody paid me in. I don't know who it was, as it was an anonymous donation. I like to tinker with different parts of machines. A couple of days ago, I made a machine that could go up into the air and stay there. It was amazing!" He said this with a sparkle in his eyes, like he was reliving the moment. "I guess somebody heard about it, and they thought that it would be good if I went to Mrs. Hearther's. We got an envelope with the money needed and an anonymous letter telling us that they heard about what I made, and they wanted to help out so I could further my education."

"Wow! That sounds really cool," I replied, fascinated. All of these kids had stories about what they wanted to do, and I was over here, having not even the slightest clue of what I wanted to study. My worries started flooding back. What if I didn't pick a science to study? Would they kick me out? Would it go back to the way life was, the way it used to be? I voiced my concerns, in case they had any idea of what I could do, or what would happen if I didn't choose.

"I am sure that once we get a tour of the school and see what the different classes entail, you will find the right choice for you," said Amanda confidently. I wanted to believe her, but my mind was telling me otherwise. I decided to try to take my mind off of the dark thoughts, and looked out the window. The train station was long gone, and in its place was a sea of trees, flooding past us. If I remembered correctly from my studies, there was only one forest as flourishing as this in all of Tarenburg: The Forest Lush. For some reason that nobody can explain, The Forest Lush's leaves were a rich, green color all year round. Even when the snows covered the grounds at the end of the year, this forest was like an oasis in a desert of white. Some people say it was haunted, but I refused to believe that. I rested my head against the window, letting the green atmosphere take me away. My eyes started to become heavy as I began to unwind. The past few hours started running through my head, like a movie. I found myself drifting off to sleep, with one thought in my head. Had I made the right choice?

I woke up to the sound of cheering all around me. I jolted up, afraid that something had happened.

"What's going on?" I asked, still somewhat groggy.

"Come on! Come on!" screamed Amanda, pulling me to my feet. I blinked rapidly and shook my head back and forth, trying to force myself awake. She pulled me to the window, and I immediately saw what all of the other kids are screaming about. The train track was running on the edge of the water, toward a giant structure. I didn't even have to ask what it was. I looked over to Rohan, who had put his book on his seat. His face was pressed against the window, wide-eyed, and smiling gleefully. We had arrived at Mrs. Hearther's School of Sciences.

CHAPTER FOUR

I T LOOKED AMAZING, ALMOST MAGICAL! FIVE TALL, MAJESTIC STONE spires circled upwards into the clouds, as if reaching toward the heavens, the one in the middle being the tallest. The water surrounding a portion of the school was glistening in the morning glow, the sun bouncing off of the surface. It was easily ten times the size of our house at home! As the train approached, I could feel the anticipation in the room growing, but also, I could sense a little bit of worry. I could tell that Rohan was nervous about whether or not he was going to fit in.

"Hey," I said, going to sit next to him. "Everything is going to be okay. They are going to love you at Mrs. Hearther's. Don't be so nervous." He looked up toward me in shock, like I had just read his future.

"How did you know that I was nervous? I never said that I was," he replied, startled.

"I don't know," I replied, honestly. "I guess I could just sense it off of you. Just like I can sense that Amanda is really, really, really excited."

"Well of course you know that," she replied, without taking her eyes off of the fast approaching school. "It's the only thing I've been talking about."

"Well, yes. But I am also getting a hint of nervousness in you as well. You don't want to upset your family. Because middle-class citizens rarely get to go," I said, slowly. How did I know all of this? It was like somebody was feeding me what to say, but I didn't know where the voice was coming from. It was like I could read their thoughts, their wants, their needs. It was like magic.

"Yes," she said skeptically. "That is what I am thinking." Both Rohan and Amanda looked at each other, then at me curiously.

"Hey, don't look at me! I don't know what is going on either," I told them, shrugging. I wanted to say something else, to reassure them that I am still me, but before I could, a voice came onto the intercom.

"Hello students," it said. A shrill ringing noise cut in and the three of us put our hands to our ears. It went on for a couple of seconds, until finally, it died down.

"What was that!" yelled somebody from another cart.

"We apologize for that," said the voice again, this time normal. "We are about to arrive at Mrs. Hearther's School of the Sciences in Tarenburg. When the train stops, exit in an orderly fashion and line up along the train outside. Thank you, and enjoy Mrs. Hearther's." The intercom turned off, and we began talking again. After a couple of minutes, the train stopped. We picked up our bags, and left our room, attempting to walk through the sea of people getting off of the train.

Eventually, we all got off and lined up outside the train. In front of us, there was a giant cobblestone archway that led to some sort of courtyard. A giant green sign was posted on the top of the archway. The sign looked familiar, but I couldn't put my finger on where I had seen it before. Then, I remembered. That symbol had been on the back of the invitation I had received. I fished into my pocket and pulled out the letter. I flipped it around and compared the symbols to each other. Just as I had thought, they were the same. But I still didn't know what the five symbols meant. I also noticed a sentence written under the symbol. It read: "Where magic and science are one." What did that mean?

The courtyard was enclosed by giant walls reaching upward, forming a giant circle. There was a tile floor, with mismatched orange and yellow tiles. Some of them looked dirty and worn out, like they had been there since the beginning, and some of them looked brand new. A couple of small trees in pots lined the walls. Once we were all lined up, I counted to see how many people were here. The invitation had said that there were twenty-four other people, meaning there were twenty-five in total. I counted down the line of teenagers, but I only counted twenty-three, including me. I recounted just to make sure, but once again, there were only twenty-three people. Where could the other two people be? I looked to see if I could recognize anybody in the line that I saw while I was boarding the train, and when I finished, I realized that there were in fact two people missing. The two kids in the train cart over to us. The rowdy, misbehaved ones. The Mallery twins. Were they still partying in their room?

I was about to say something, when I heard voices inside the train, some yelling and arguing. We all turned around to see what the commotion was and saw one of the instructors pull out two kids by their ears. To no one's surprise, it was the Mallery twins. The instructor pushed them into line, much to their complaint. They rubbed their ears in pain, but none of the teachers addressed the issue. The woman who pulled the Mallery twins out walked to the front of us to address us all.

"Now that that has been taken care of, let the introductions begin. First off, I want to say thank you all for coming here today. All twenty-five of you showed up, which is a rare thing to happen. Welcome to Mrs. Hearther's School of the Sciences!" A cheer erupted from the line, and I found myself joining in it as well. After a few seconds of clapping, whistling, and yelling, the woman put up her hands as a signal for us to quiet down.

"But before we start with introductions, I want to say that Mrs. Hearther's is more than a school for science. Yes, we study science, but not in the way that you think. See, science has two sides, the physical," she gestures to a little plant on the ground, "and the magical." Magical? What does that even mean? I saw the other kids have the same confusion as me. The instructor smiled. "We here at Mrs. Hearther's study the magical side of science, the part of it which not many people believe is true."

"Hey!" called a voice from the line. I looked over to see that it is one of the twins. "I don't believe in this magical mumbo jumbo. I mean, do you seriously want us to believe that magic is real? What about the scientists?" he said slowly, mockingly. "Can I leave now? It sounds like you guys are on something crazy right now. By the way, you mind telling me what exactly you're on?" After a few seconds of silence, he forced a smile, one side higher than the other.

"Uh, no sir, I believe you have come to the wrong place for that. See, you, along with many other people in the world are one of the non-believers. Do you want to see proof?" she asked.

"Well duh," he replied playfully, crossing his arms and rolling his eyes. Promptly, the instructor pointed to a plant, and stared it down. Suddenly, out of nowhere, the plant started to grow and bloom into a beautiful poppy. What? What just happened? How is that even possible? The courtyard turned into a form of chaos, everybody in a confused panic.

"What was that?"

"How is that possible?"

"What if they try to do what they did on that plant, on us?" But how did she do that? It was like she told it to grow, and it listened to her. It was just like the sign said. Science and magic are one.

"And that's not all you can do," she said, trying to calm the chaos. "If you would like another demonstration, why don't you follow me." She turned right and started walking down the sidewalk, toward the side of the building, where there was nothing but a single tree. "There are dangers in this world, from our myths and legends. Because of that, we need to protect Tarenburg as well as the people in it. This is how we do it." She took a deep breath, and what she did next left us all in shock. She jumped up into the air and as she came down, she hit the ground with her fist, and suddenly, a shockwave was sent throughout the ground toward the tree, splitting the earth in two, revealing the roots of the tree. We all stumbled back, shaken from the force of the blow. She raised her arms, and the roots from the tree sprouted out of the ground, forming an octopus around her. Splinters flew everywhere, and we covered our faces so as to not get hit.

She then proceeded to fling her arms into the air, and then shot the roots into the sky, like spears, and then they came crashing down, penetrating the ground around her. She pointed her hands to the top of the tree, and the leaves all fell off and flew over to her hands. They twirled around her arms, forming leaf extensions, both moving in the wind, and to her command. She reached her arms out, and the leaves intertwined around the tree. Defying physics, the leaves picked up the trunk, and threw it into the air. She shot her arms out, releasing her grasp on the leaves, letting them fly freely. As the tree came crashing down on top of her, she raised her right hand, forming a spear, and sliced the trunk in half, saving herself from near death. Then, just like in the beginning, she took a deep breath, lowered her hands, and bowed to the tree. We all stood there, wide-eyed, mouths open in shock.

"These are just some of the things that you can do with the magical side of science," she said, turning to face us, a big grin on her face. "Each aspect that we teach here has its own skills. But be warned, most of the people here on Tarenburg don't know that magic exists. There are two groups of people, the church and the scientists, and you are either one or the other. Then, there is a fine line in between, one that has aspects of the church and science. That fine line is magic, and if you go around telling random people about it, our world will be in danger. You all have been carefully selected to help keep the balance in our world. You will learn more tomorrow, but for now, you will be assigned to your dorms. Make sure you get a good night's rest, as you'll need it for tomorrow. My name is Eliza Hearther, and welcome to my school of the sciences."

CHAPTER FIVE

AFTER MRS. HEARTHER'S DEMONSTRATION, SHE WALKED THE mouth-gaping, eyes-wide children that we were to the dorm rooms. We walked back to where the train dropped us off, and headed under the grand arches to the courtyard. The courtyard was massive, with kids ranging from sixteen to twenty, all practicing their magic. As we walked past them, I observed some of them doing what Mrs. Hearther did, and some of them were doing things I couldn't even fathom. I wanted to stay longer to watch what they were doing, but Mrs. Hearther kept walking and turned right, to a building with a sign that read SIXTEEN-YEAR-OLDS. We walked in through the front doors and were presented with hallways on either side of us, and a grand, red-carpeted staircase in front, presumably leading to more rooms. She turned left and walked us down the hallway. A couple doors down, she stopped.

"This room, along with the next six rooms, are for the middle and lower-class students. You can choose whichever room you want. It will lock automatically behind you and there is a key for the door inside. You have nothing else to do today, so you may stay in your dorms. Dinner will be delivered to your rooms at seven. Breakfast is at eight A.M. sharp, in the building labeled 'Dining Hall.' If you walk out of this building and take a right, it is that building there. Remember, eight A.M. on the dot. No later. After breakfast, I will meet with all of you to show you around campus." Mrs. Hearther gestured to the rooms, signaling for the appropriate students to go inside. I waved goodbye to Amanda and Rohan as they walked inside their rooms.

Mrs. Hearther then turned around and pointed up the stairs, "Your rooms are up there on the second story. Just like down here, you can choose whichever room you would like, just as long as it doesn't have a marker on it. The markers have the room number, the name of the person staying, as well as their age. You will be receiving your marker tomorrow afternoon. Enjoy your stay, and remember, eight A.M. sharp, dining hall." And just like that, she turned around and walked out the front doors, letting us go on our own. We all walked up the stairs and went to find our rooms. I strolled down the hallway, trying to find a room that didn't have a marker on it, and eventually, I found one: Room 16-228. I walked in and shut the door behind me. I heard the lock click into place as I set my bag down on the table with the key on it. It was a normal looking key, golden with the numbers 16-228 engraved on the side of it.

The room was simple, with a table as soon as you walked in, and a mirror above it. In the back, there was the bed and a nightstand next to it with a light and journal with a pen on top of it. A bathroom was located behind the wall with the desk. There was a window behind the bed, overlooking the courtyard. I opened the curtains to see the view I got, and was immediately happy with my decision. Outside my window was a view of the entire courtyard. I could see all of the other kids practicing their magic. I was going to like it here.

I took my clothes and placed them in the drawers of the nightstand. I put my toothbrush in the bathroom. My watch read 6:30, so I had a little bit of time until dinner. I lay on my bed and looked out the window, watching the other people. One day, I would be as good as them. After what seemed like only five minutes, I heard a knock at my door. I checked my watch and it read 7 o'clock on the dot. I walked to the door and opened it. There was a tray on the floor, with my food in it. I peeked my head out of my room and saw all of the other kids coming out of their rooms to collect their dinner. Their dishes all looked similar to mine. I picked it up and took it inside to enjoy, closing the door behind me. The dinner was a simple potato, but nonetheless, it was still delicious. I plopped myself on my bed and looked out the window to see if I could see anybody else practicing, but they were all in the process of going inside. I closed the blinds and ate in silence. After I finished eating, I noticed a note saying that after I was done with my food, I should put the tray outside my door to be picked up during the night. I was exhausted after my long journey today. I couldn't believe that just this morning, I was still in the comfort of my house, with Mom, Dad, and Tinna. They were probably really angry at me. But once I helped the world, they would see that it was needed for me. As my mind started to wander, I lowered myself into the bed and fell asleep.

I woke up at around 7:30, and started to get ready for the day. I brushed my teeth, showered, got changed, and headed downstairs to the dining hall. I saw Rohan and Amanda standing by the front door to the dining hall. I ran over to them.

"Hey guys," I called them. "How were your rooms?" They didn't say anything back. They just looked down at their shoes and turned away from me. "What's wrong?"

"Look around," Amanda whispered. "Upper-class students don't talk to middle or lower-class kids." I looked around, and sure enough, almost everybody in the courtyard was giving us looks.

"I don't care about them. I want to be your friend." Once again, they didn't say anything and turned away from me. What was going on? Yesterday, they wanted to be my friends. What happened? Before I could say anything else, Mrs. Hearther opened up the doors to the dining hall, and everybody rushed inside. I decided to worry about it later, and walked inside with everybody else. Once I walked into the room, I realized how massive it was. Giant chandeliers came down from the ceiling, shining light onto the many tables scattered across the room. I was about to follow Rohan and Amanda, but then remembered what they had said earlier. Upper-class kids don't sit with middle or lower-class people. I turned around and went to sit with the upper-class kids. It wasn't as exciting. I kept to myself the whole time but noticed people staring at me, and whispering to their friends. The Mallery twins were doing most of the talking, attempting to flirt with two girls.

Shortly after breakfast, Mrs. Hearther called all of us to the side for our tour. She took us to the back of the dining hall, where there was another grand archway. We went under it and Mrs. Hearther turned right, down a hallway that said SIXTEEN-YEAR-OLDS.

"Here at Mrs. Hearther's School of the Sciences, we study engineering, zoology, botany, astronomy, and psychology. Those are the first classrooms here. You will be choosing only one class to take. Make sure you choose wisely, because once you perform your first action in a certain field, that is the field you will be working in for your whole life, and you cannot use magic from any of the other sciences. Of course, we also provide your core classes, math, language, history, as well as some other magical lessons. Those classrooms are in the back of this building. Later tonight, you will get a schedule sent to your room with your classes and room number." Mrs. Hearther stopped in front of the first door in the building.

"This classroom is for engineering." I looked to see if I could find Rohan. Eventually, I found him and I saw his eyes were wide with excitement. This was what he had been dreaming about since the second he got on the train. "This is our engineering instructor Mr. Ringly." She pointed to a small, round man, with big boxy glasses in front of a chalkboard with what looked like a lot of calculations. Some of them I recognized from what I had been taught being homeschooled, but most of it was completely new to me. "Mr. Ringly, could you please give us a demonstration?" He nodded and picked up a little machine. It was made out of mostly metal parts, but it had something else to it. Not physical, but something magical about it was jumping out, making it seem even more special than it already was. He threw it into the air, and I expected it to fall back down into his hands, but it just stayed there, suspended in midair, kind of like what Rohan said he was able to do. Then, he moved his hands back and forth, and the machine followed it. He moved his hands in circles, and so did the machine. It was like they were one. It was amazing. I heard a little "Woah" come out of Rohan's mouth.

"Thank you Mr. Ringly," said Mrs. Hearther. "Now let's move on." We walked across the hallway to the next classroom. "This is the zoology classroom. This is Mrs. Hiley." Mrs. Hiley was a bubbly, tall, blonde woman who looked like she was in her early thirties. She was hunched over a squirrel, examining it. As she heard us walking in, she perked her head up. "Could you please give us a demonstration?" asked Mrs. Hearther.

"Sure," Mrs. Hiley happily replied. She turned back toward the squirrel and stared into its eyes. "Jump three times," she said. Not even a second after she said that, the squirrel got up on its hind legs and jumped not once, not twice, but just like Mrs. Hiley asked, three times. "Now, that time, I said the command out loud, but you can also use a special mind link if you get advanced enough to talk to it directly through your mind. If you can do that, it can also talk to you, and you will be able to understand each other."

"Thank you," said Mrs. Hearther. While that was cool, I'm not sure that is what I wanted to study. After all, Roger was already taking zoology. I wanted to do something different than him. We moved out of the classroom and went to the next one.

"This is the astronomy classroom," said Mrs. Hearther. I turned toward Amanda, and I saw a giant smile plastered on her face. "This classroom has an open ceiling because, well, it's astronomy. Astronomy is taught by Ms. Wesmirth." Ms. Wesmirth was a short, elderly, kind looking woman, who was examining a chart of what looked like constellations. This demonstration was the coolest by far. Ms. Wesmirth looked up to the clouds, and suddenly, a beam of light appeared where she was standing, and as soon as it appeared, it went away. There was no trace of where she had gone. A thought crept into my mind as she did this. I tried to push it away, but it kept persisting and nagging at me. That was kind of like what happened with Dad. But no, he couldn't know about magic. Could he? Did he study astronomy? Before I could think about it further, I heard a voice behind us. We all turned around and saw Ms. Wesmirth walking through the front door of the classroom, the very one we had walked through just seconds ago.

"By learning the magic of astronomy, you will be able to transport yourself to any place in the world, just as long as you can picture it in your mind," Ms. Wesmirth told us.

"Thank you for that demonstration," said Mrs. Hearther, walking out the door and to the next classroom. We followed her. "The next room is for botany, but I am going to skip that room, since I already gave you a demonstration yesterday morning. But I will introduce you to your teacher, Mr. Ferod." Mr. Ferod was a tall, lanky, middle-aged man who was looking over some plants, taking samples. He waved to us and Mrs. Hearther waved back. We moved on to the next room. I started biting my lip and fidgeting with my fingers. This was the last of the sciences, and I still hadn't found one that I wanted to study. Hopefully the next one would suit me.

"This next room is the room for psychology. The teacher is Mr. Poli." Mr. Poli was of average height, with a bright blue suit and a yellow tie. "Could you please give us a demonstration, Mr. Poli?" asked Mrs. Hearther, as we walked into the room.

"Certainly," replied Mr. Poli. He looked around at us, as if looking for someone in particular. Please don't be me. "You there, with the pale skin. Could you please come up here?" Of course he picked me. I walked up tentatively, scared about what he might do to me. "You don't need to be shy," he said, giving me a smile. "You'll be okay," he reassured me. "Now stand here, right in front of me." I did as he said and looked right into his eyes.

"Now, think about something that has special value to you. Something you care for a lot." The first thing that popped into my head was Tinna. I thought of her, alone at home, with nobody to be with. Sitting in her room, playing with her dolls, having to take care of herself and having nothing to entertain herself with. Mom and Dad wouldn't take any attention to her. She was probably miserable. Then, Mr. Poli said the unthinkable.

"You're thinking about your sister, Tinna. Up in her room with just her toys. Your parents don't love you. They don't take the time to care for you," he said. I felt a tear forming in my eye, but I forced it to go back. I nodded my head.

"That's not real!" called somebody from the audience. What do you know, it was one of the Mallery twins. "You probably just read his file and that's how you know that."

"Oh, I assure you, it's real. What's your name?" Mr. Poli asked calmly.

"My name's Harold Mallery. Why don't you do one of your 'mind tricks' on me then?" he said smugly.

"Very well," said Mr. Poli, sighing. Mr. Poli looked right into his eyes, staring him down. "Harold, sleep," Mr. Poli said coolly. Suddenly, Harold dropped to the ground. We all gasped, circling around him to see if he was okay.

"He is alright," Mr. Poli said, reassuring us. "But the fun has just begun. Everybody move out of the way please." We all cleared a path for Mr. Poli to get to Harold. Mr. Poli once again stared him down, but this time he didn't say anything. He backed away, and motioned for us to do the same. After a few seconds, Harold opened his eyes and jumped up, gasping. He then proceeded to jump on top of the table, screaming at the top of his lungs, making a fool of himself. He then jumped down and ran out of the room, yelling like a fire truck down the hallway. Everybody laughed, and even Mrs. Hearther let out a little giggle. I smiled. I think I knew which science I wanted to study.

CHAPTER SIX

LATER THAT NIGHT, AS I WAS LYING IN BED, I HEARD A SMALL KNOCK on the door, and a piece of paper slipped under the crack. It shot across the carpet floor and slid to the side of the bed. I turned over and picked it up, opening the folded paper. On it was my schedule, as promised. There was a list of eight events, each an hour long—breakfast, language, history, beginners' magical geography, lunch, math, beginners' magical beings, and lastly, psychology.

I was in my room thinking about what I had learned today. Did Dad study astronomy? Did he know about this magic? Is that what happened that morning? It was almost as if he had vanished into thin air, just like what had happened when Ms. Wesmirth demonstrated it. But no, it couldn't be. Dad was deeply rooted in the church. It didn't make any sense. I fell asleep thinking about these thoughts.

The next day started the same as the last. I got ready for my day, and then went downstairs to the dining hall. Once again, I saw Amanda and Rohan standing in the corner, talking to themselves. I wanted to go over and talk to them, and I started to, but then I remembered what they had said. Something must have happened from when we exited the train to yesterday morning. When we first met, they were happy to be my friends. I went to stand at the edge of the courtyard, leaning against one of the giant pots holding the trees.

I watched the other kids practice their magic. As I was watching two older kids practice their botany on some nearby plants, I noticed out of the corner of my eye two people walking up to me. I looked over to see who it was, and my heart started racing. Why were they coming over to me? Why me?

"Hey little guy," said one of the Mallery twins, coming to stand beside me. "Who dropped a bucket of bleach on you?"

"Good one Bruce!" said Harold, cackling. This attracted the attention of the other kids in the courtyard. They stopped whatever they were doing, and turned to face us, quiet as mice. I suddenly became very uncomfortable with all of their eyes staring right at me. "Go back to where you belong, alien freak!" Harold called. My lip started quivering and I felt my eyes start to dampen. Nobody had ever humiliated me in my life because I looked different. Amanda had said that other people would be mean to me, and I figured I could handle it, but I didn't know that they would be this mean. Everybody kept staring, unblinking. Some of them were looking at me in disgust, like I didn't belong here. Some of them were looking at me in pity, and some of them were just watching for the fun of it. They looked between the Mallery twins and me, most likely playing in their head how this situation would end. In my mind, it would end with me running off crying with everybody else laughing behind me, Harold's and Bruce's laughs being the loudest. Just the thought of that made my heart slow, my eyes water even more. I turned away to face the wall, not wanting them to see my face.

"Oh, what are you going to do?" asks Harold. "Are you going to go cry to your mommy?" he said tauntingly. Just then, a fire ignited inside of me. Rage started to build up in me. I tried to dampen it, but it was too strong, and I let it take over me. I had to find something to insult him with, something personal. Something that would hurt him. And just then, I thought of the perfect thing.

"At least I have a mom to go cry to." Suddenly, the entire courtyard got quiet. Bruce and Harold took a step back, and their eyes narrowed. I had just made a huge mistake. I tried to put on a brave face, and give them a little smirk, but it came off as a wince.

"What did you just say to me?" Harold asked.

"Nothing," I replied, my voice raising a couple of octaves. I started walk-ing away from them, not wanting to be around them anymore. I got a couple of feet away from them when I felt a tug on my shirt. I turned around and before I could even react, I saw something flying toward my face at the speed of a rocket. Before I knew what was happening, a sharp pain encompassed my entire face. I was thrown to the ground, face against the tile. I spit, and found that blood came out. I turned around slowly, not wanting to damage anything else. I looked up and saw Harold twisting his wrist, and giving me a giant devilish grin.

"You got him good," observed Bruce, patting Harold on the shoulder. Bruce wore the same maniacal grin as his twin. I took a couple of deep breaths and did my best to stand up. I crawled onto my knees and slowly looked around me at the other kids. Now, most of them were looking at me in disgust. I saw a few faces of worry, but not enough to combat the hate. I picked one foot up and gingerly placed it flat on the ground. I did the same with the other foot, and started to slowly get up. After a few seconds, I was on my feet again. I felt the side of my face, and I felt something sticky on the side of it. I took my hand away and was shocked to see a bright red liquid on my fingers, dripping down, staining the courtyard floor. My head was spinning, and I had to close my eyes to recover. Harold really hit me hard. Just then, for a second, my mind cleared for a thought to come through: Harold punched me. The fire reignited inside of me, and before I knew what I was doing, I picked my hand up, and closed my fingers around each other, making a fist.

I brought my hand back and swung it toward Harold. All of my rage and sadness bottled up into my hand, and as I brought it forward, I felt it come in contact with skin.

"Oof!" yelled Harold, stepping back, covering his stomach with his hand. He looked down at his chest, then back at me, breathing heavily. "Oh, you just made a huge mistake," he said walking toward me. Bruce followed him, and I tried to retreat, but a group of some of the other kids blocked my path. I was forced to turn around and face the Mallery twins. I forced my shaky hands to protect my face, and through the cracks of my fingers, I saw Harold and Bruce walk menacingly over to me. Just then, I heard the creaking of wood coming from the direction of the dining hall. The door opened, revealing Mrs. Hearther. She spread the doors wide open, with a giant smile on her face.

"Hello everybody!" she called. "Are you ready for—" She didn't get to finish her sentence as she saw the scene in the courtyard, me huddled in a corner, face bloody, with the Mallery twins approaching me. Everybody turned their head to look at her. Her eyes widened in shock, and then narrowed in anger. She stormed over to us, and I tensed up even more than I already was, ready for a beating, physical or verbal. First, she walked to the Mallery twins, and stood right in front of them. I thought the Mallery twins were tall, but Mrs. Hearther seemed to tower over the both of them.

"What is going on here? And don't try to play dumb with me," she criticized them. I could almost see fumes coming out of her ears.

"Well, Mrs. Hearther," Harold started in a calm and collected voice, completely different from his tone two minutes ago. "My brother and I were minding our own business, when this kid here walks up to us."

"Yeah," picked up Bruce. "We greeted him and were very nice to him, but this kid just insulted our mom! Well, our lack of a mom." His eyes started squinting in concentration. His eyes moved back and forth, eyelids opening and closing, like his eyes were having a seizure. Mrs. Hearther looked at him funny, and I could tell that she doesn't believe them.

"What are you trying to do?" she asked, curious.

"What do you mean?" Bruce asked, panting, eyes still spasming.

"Okay, I can tell you're lying," Mrs. Hearther said, looking unimpressed. "How do you explain Jeremy's bloody face?" she asked, motioning toward me. I looked down, not wanting to be the center of attention.

"Well, uh, you see," started Harold.

"Whatever. I don't want to hear it. Report to my office immediately. Both of you. I don't want to hear another word out of either of you. I will be right with you." As the Mallery twins were walking away toward the dorms, Harold turned around and put his index and middle fingers to his eyes and then pointed them to me, as if he would be watching me.

"What was that?" I heard Harold whispering, criticizing Bruce.

"What do you mean? I was trying to make myself cry. Like you taught me!"

"Dumb idiot! I told you you look stupid doing it and to never do it again. This is why I'm the leader!" I suppressed a laugh, and turned to face Mrs. Hearther. Her face looked a little kinder than it was with the Mallery twins, but she still looked annoyed.

"Let's get you to the nurse's office," she said. "On the way there, you can tell me what happened." She took me through the doors of the dining hall. "Breakfast is ready!" she called behind her. I heard the other kids start to run into the room, and head straight to the buffet. I walked past them, following directly behind Mrs. Hearther. Once we exited the back doors of the dining hall, we headed straight, going under another archway, and into another hallway.

"So, do you want to tell me what happened?" she asked, looking down at me. I looked down, trying to hide my blushing. I didn't want to talk about what happened. "It's okay," Mrs. Hearther said. "I know all about the twins. What happened probably wasn't your fault. You're not in trouble. I just want to know what happened." I sighed, relenting.

"Okay. The Mallery twins approached me and told me that I looked different. They were making fun of me, just because my skin is lighter than everybody else's. I wanted to get back at them for what they said." I stopped, debating whether I should keep going. If I told her what I said, I could be in big trouble. But if I didn't tell her, and she found out, I would be in even bigger trouble. I decided to tell her. "I did insult their mom. I just wanted to get back at them for everything that they said to me. After I said that, Harold punched me in the face, sending me to the ground. I got up, and hit him back, right in the chest." I smiled, remembering the shocked and hurt face of Harold. "And then they started approaching me, both of them. I tried to run away, but some of the other kids blocked my path. I don't know what I would have done if you weren't there." I looked up at Mrs. Hearther and I saw her face scrunched up, as if she was thinking deeply about something. After a few seconds, she started talking again.

"What you did wasn't right. You should never insult or hit another student." I looked down, too ashamed to look at her. "But I will admit, you got them good." I looked up at her, confused. She smiled down at me, and I couldn't help myself from grinning back. "I don't think they will be messing with you for a while now. And I'm proud of you for standing up for yourself. Let's just get you cleaned up." We stopped at a door, and she motioned me inside.

The room was filled with all kinds of medical equipment. The walls were lined with cabinets full of medicines. An examination table was placed in the middle of the room, with dark red cushions, and milk-white drawers full of common medical supplies. I could see a stethoscope, some needles and syringes, and more things I couldn't name. There was a tall woman hunched over a desk, reviewing some papers.

"This is Dr. Golpel. She will take good care of you," said Mrs. Hearther. Dr. Golpel looked up from her papers and greeted us with a smile.

"Hello," she said. She looked at my face, right where Harold hit me. "Looks like you got hurt. Would you mind coming to sit down on the exam table so I can look at you?" I tentatively walked over, and jumped onto the bed. I took a deep breath as she rolled her chair over to look at me.

"Knock knock," said a voice at the door. I opened my eyes to see who it was. When I did see him, I was immediately filled with joy. I tried to smile, but found that it hurts, so I resorted to waving.

"I heard about what happened," said Roger, walking into the room. "I hope I'm not interrupting anything."

"Nope. We were just finishing up," said Dr. Golpel, bringing a light to check my face one more time. I saw something in Roger's hand, a tray of some sort. He noticed me staring, and smiled.

"I figured you would be hungry, so I brought you some pancakes from breakfast." My mood went from happy to overjoyed with the sound of those words. Dr. Golpel rolled away, and told me that I was good to go.

"Just make sure you don't do anything too intensive for the next couple of days. Be careful with your magic," she said. I nodded in understanding and hopped off the table. I ran over to Roger, and embraced him in a giant bear hug.

"It's good to have you here," he said, hugging me back. "I didn't know if you would get in or not. How are Mom and Dad? Is Tinna okay?" he asked, handing me the tray of food.

"Mom and Dad are okay. They still ignore us, like before. They didn't want me to come here, so I snuck away," I replied, in between mouthfuls of pancakes. "I tried to take care of Tinna. I played with her, made her meals, and took care of her. I'm worried about her, and if she'll be okay without me there." I sighed and closed my eyes, thinking back to home. I walked through the door, and out into the hallway. Roger followed me.

"I'm sorry, Jeremy," he replied. "Tinna will be okay. She is strong and can take care of herself." He embraced me with another hug. I could feel and sense all of his love and care for me. But also, I could feel another emotion buried deep down. I didn't know how to describe it. It was like a raging forest fire, tearing its way through Roger's heart. It was like disgust, but more powerful. It was like burning agony.

"You are going to fit in perfectly here. Which science are you going to study?" he asked me.

"I want to study psychology," I replied, trying to shake the strange feeling away. "Mr. Poli did a really cool demonstration, and I want to learn more about it."

"Sounds cool. See you around," he said, giving me a wave. I tried to sense his feelings again, but this time, the feeling of loathing was gone, only love. It was as if after I told him that I wanted to study psychology, the feeling just went away.

"Bye," I said to him. He walked away, down the hallway, presumably to his class. Something was off about him. I couldn't quite tell what it was yet, but I was going to figure it out. When I learn more about psychology, I would hopefully be able to strengthen what abilities I already seem to have, and I will be able to help him. And then, I will be able to help the world.

CHAPTER SEVEN

THE DAY SEEMED TO GO ON FOREVER UNTIL FINALLY IT WAS THE afternoon and time for psychology class. I ran through the hallway toward Mr. Poli's classroom, and went to find a seat in the front.

"Good afternoon, Jeremy," Mr. Poli greeted me. "How is your head?"

"It's doing better. Thanks," I replied. Mr. Poli was writing something on the board, but I couldn't tell what it was yet. It looked like a drawing of the human brain. "I believe you, along with five others, decided to take this class," he said, after he was done creating the diagram. I sat down and looked around me. There was nothing much in the classroom, save for a few models of the human body. I suppose that was because psychology has everything to do with the mind, and there aren't many physical properties to it. One by one, the other kids started walking into the room, two girls and three boys. I didn't recognize any of them. They all took seats scattered around the room. None of them sat in the same row as me.

"Okay. We are going to start with the basics. Psychology is all about getting into the other person's head. Some people may be harder than others, and some may be willing to let you in. But you have to assert your control over them. Once you are inside of their head, you are their master. Let's start with the frontal lobe," Mr. Poli stated, pointing to a spot on the diagram.

"The frontal lobe is the part of the brain that controls functions like thinking and judgement. In order to go into a person's mind and control them, you need to transfer your thoughts into their brain, mainly their frontal lobe.

"It can also help to tap into their cerebellum," he stated, pointing to another picture on the board. "The cerebellum is the part of the brain that controls things like movement and speech. Picture the brain as something you really like, something you can't live without, like a pet, or a type of food." Instantly I thought of Tinna, and how much I cared for her.

"Now, pretend like somebody took that thing away from you. You now want to reach out and take it back. Reach out and take control of that object, or in a more literal sense, their brain and willpower. Focus more on the frontal lobe and cerebellum, and you should be able to do this with ease.

"Now let's practice. I want to see where each of you are at, so I can help you individually become the best you can be. I want you all to pick a partner, and try to do something simple. Maybe command them to spin in a circle three times." Mr. Poli went to his desk, and sat back watching us trying to find a partner. Everybody frantically chose a partner, until there was just me and a girl left. The girl looked around, and the other kids gave her looks of pity. She sighed and walked over to me.

"Okay. Do you want to go first, or me?" asked the girl, shyly.

"You can go first," I replied, trying to sound friendly. I took a step back and waited. She stared into my eyes. We held that stare for about thirty seconds, then she let out her breath, and sighed.

"I give up," she said, looking down.

"Don't give up," said Mr. Poli. "Most people don't get it on their first try. Why don't you try, Jeremy?" I nodded my head and stared into her eyes. I pictured Tinna, and how I would feel if somebody took her away. Frantically, I tried to reach out and take her back and after a few seconds, I started to feel a tingling sensation in the back of my head, like someone else was in there. "Spin three times," I said in my head. Suddenly, the girl in front of me gasped, and started moving her legs in a spinning motion. She spun once. The other kids stopped what they were doing and looked over at us. She spun twice. Mr. Poli sat up in his chair and leaned forward, wonder in his eyes. She spun one more time, making it three, just like I had commanded. Then, we both gasped, and wobbled back, a little off balance. I widened my eyes, and sat down. How did I do that?

"It looks like we have somebody with inborn talent," said Mr. Poli, shocked. He stood up out of his chair, and walked over to me. He put his hand on my shoulder. "Just like your brother," he said smiling. I looked up at him and smiled back. And then I realized something. I could ask Mr. Poli about Roger. Since he was a psychology expert, he should know that something was off.

"Can I talk to you after class?" I asked him.

"Sure," he replied, still smiling.

After class, I went up to his desk and asked him the burning question.

"I met with Roger earlier this morning. We were talking and everything was okay, but I sensed a feeling that I have never sensed something off of him. I can't quite describe it, but I could just tell that something was wrong. I know I've never felt that emotion from him before. I can't put a word to it, but it almost didn't feel human. Can you think of anything that is happening?" He looked a little shocked, but then recovered himself.

"I don't think anything is wrong. Remember, you haven't seen him in a while. I'm sure everything is fine," he replied, trying to reassure me.

"But you don't know Roger like I do. This doesn't feel like him," I insisted.

"We will look into the matter, but I assure you, you have nothing to worry about. It was probably just first day jitters." He was hiding something. I didn't know what it was, but I would find out and help Roger. I didn't ask any more questions. I just nodded my head, and returned to the courtyard to watch the other kids practice before dinner.

As I entered the courtyard, I slunk along the perimeter, trying to stay out of sight. I didn't want anybody to see me after the whole ordeal this morning. As I walked along the edge, I watched two older kids practicing psychology on each other, making the other lift a certain number of fingers in the air, or jump a certain number of times. I started to walk closer to them, to see if I could get a better look. As I was walking, I started nearing the edge of the courtyard, and was about to keep walking, when suddenly, one of the tiles clacked under my foot. I stumbled and almost fell to the ground before getting back up.

I looked down at the tile and saw that it was slightly lower than the others. I took my foot off of it, and it shot back into place, seamlessly blending in with the other tiles. Tentatively, I placed my foot back down on the tile, and just like last time, it lowered slightly, and when it did, it sounded like gears shifting, kind of like a pressure plate.

I looked around to see if it did anything, but everything looked exactly the same. All of the kids were still practicing their magic. Nothing was out of place. Taking my foot off of the tile, I started walking again. It was probably nothing. But not one second after my foot left the tile, a second tile fell, making another clicking noise. Why were there two pressure plates? And right next to each other. Maybe it was a pattern. Maybe I had to step on them in a certain way, and then something would happen. Taking my right foot off of the tile, I placed it back onto the first one, and then my left foot on the second tile. I heard the gears start to turn again, and then after a few seconds, a click.

For a few seconds, nothing happened, but then, right in front of my eyes, the three tiles in front of the two I was standing on retracted into the floor, revealing a staircase going downward. What was this? How long had this been here? Did anybody else know about it? I could go back to my room now and forget this ever happened. I wouldn't risk getting in trouble for going somewhere I maybe wasn't supposed to. Or, I could go now and see what mysteries the school was hiding. Without a second thought, I let curiosity take over me, and walked downward, to wherever this took me. Right as I was under the floor, the tiles closed above me, and I was plunged into darkness. I was stuck!

Banging on the roof, I called for help, but nobody came. They probably wouldn't even be able to hear me. Of course this happened to me. Why didn't I just leave it alone? Why did I have to come down here? There was probably some magical axe killer here, ready to magic me to death. I would have to find another way out.

Feeling my way around the walls, I slowly started making my way down a spiral staircase. The floor was wet, and as my feet hit the ground, the splash echoed along the walls. After a few minutes of slow progress, a light suddenly appeared. As I got lower and lower, it started to get brighter. This was my way out! I started descending faster and faster until I came to an opening in the staircase, revealing a giant cavern.

Half-finished stone pillars were holding the tunnel intact, lining the edges. Cracks snaked their way up the pillars, and some moss grew in between the crevices, somehow finding a way to live down here. I couldn't figure out how tall the structure was, but it seemed significantly taller than the distance it took to get here. What kind of magic was at play here? The entire place was somehow lit up by about two dozen lanterns around the edges. How were they kept lit? Was it magic? I looked up and around me in awe of the whole build. I had so many questions. What was this place? Was it abandoned? Why was it made? Who else knew about this?

As I walked around, trying to take it all in, I heard a whooshing sound, like when water flows out of a tap. Looking to the right side of the cavern, a stream of water ran its way behind the pillars. I would have to tell somebody about this back at the school! But how would I get back? I couldn't go the way I came, as that way was shut off. All my excitement suddenly drained from me as reality started to kick in. I was stuck in here. I would never get out. There was probably a reason this project was abandoned. The people that were building probably hadn't had time to build an exit.

But wait. I hadn't seen any bodies. Which means that nobody died down here. At least, that I know of. They must have built an emergency exit, in case something went wrong. They would be stupid if they didn't. All I had to do was find it. I walked to the edge of the water and sat down, trying to think of where I should look. After a few seconds of looking into the water, it hit me. The water was running. It had to lead somewhere! Maybe that somewhere was outside!

Jumping to my feet, I started walking along the edge of the water, trying to keep as close to it as possible, so I wouldn't lose it. The stream rounded a corner, and me with it. The water seemed to go on forever, and after about ten minutes of walking, I was about to give up and turn back to try and find another way. But what if there wasn't another way? What if this was how you were supposed to get out? I had to keep going. After a few more minutes of walking, I could smell something in the air. It smelled familiar, but I couldn't quite figure out what it was. It smelled sweet and refreshing, and it was strong. I started running toward it, and soon, I could hear chittering. There were cicadas! I was making my way to the surface! I started sprinting, and the smell became even stronger.

I rounded one more corner, and there it was—the exit. Now in a full on sprint, I dashed out of the exit and looked around me. I was in the middle of a forest. What I had smelt was the pine trees! I was free! I turned around to see the exit, and it seemed to be a cave in the side of a small hill. But how was the exit here? Wasn't I just underground? And I hadn't climbed upwards? It was probably just more magic. I didn't want to think more into it, and walked through the forest until I came to a clearing. I could see the school in the distance. I snuck up to it and slunk through the entrance, somehow going undetected and went to my room for the night. I needed some time to think. About this mysterious cavern. And more importantly, about Roger.

CHAPTER EIGHT

THE LIBRARY WAS HUGE! AS I WALKED IN THROUGH THE GRAND entrance, I was greeted with rows and rows of books, both ancient and new, big and small. The bookshelves went forward for as long as the eye could see, and upward to the roof. I wondered how they got the books on the top. Then, just as if answering my question, a bird whizzed right past me. I took a step back and gasped as the bird shot up to the ceiling. It stopped at a certain row and hovered in midair, starting at the shelf. After a few seconds, the bird took a book from the shelf and flew back down to the ground. It flew past me again and I watched its path. It went around to the side of the library, to a desk with a few kids. The bird landed next to one of them, and dropped the book in his hands. Now, I started to understand. All of the librarians must be zoologists, and the only way to get to the upper books is to ask one of them to command their bird to get it.

I went to a lectern with a giant book in the front of the building and flipped to the glossary. I moved my finger downward, trying to look for anything about what I had learned earlier. I had never known Roger to hate anything before. Mr. Poli might be right, and it might just be first day jitters and the fact that I haven't seen him in so long. But I also knew my brother, and if something had happened, he would have told me. I looked through the glossary to find books on emotions and psychology. After a few minutes of looking,

I finally came across a section about emotions in the psychology section. I memorized the row and section of the books and closed the book on the lectern, leaving it for the next person to read. I meandered through the library, making my way to the books. As I walked, I looked around me and appreciated the work that must have gone into making this place a reality. How did they acquire all of these books? I continued walking, making sure I was focusing on the numbers against the shelves, and when I came to the right section, I stopped and paid attention to the books. I rolled my finger along the spines, looking at their titles.

After some searching, I finally found the books I wanted. I made my way back to the entrance of the library, where I saw some tables to sit at. I went to one of them, and sat the books down, as well as myself. I read through the first book, which was about commanding people through psychology. It was interesting, and a book that would be very useful in the future, but not what I was looking for now. I scanned a couple more books until I came upon the one I was looking for.

This book was about different emotions people had, and why they might feel them. I looked at the glossary, containing the different emotions. Happiness, sadness, anger, distress, disgust, and so many more. I kept looking until I came upon an emotion that I had never heard of: hate. I flipped to the section about hate which was a lot longer than the other ones. After a lot of reading, I came upon something that might be useful. It said that hate, whatever it is, isn't a natural human emotion, rather, it is given to them by a creature. Nobody has seen this creature because it doesn't take a physical form. Rather, it infests different human bodies, and works through them. But that was all of the information that it gave.

Sighing, I closed the book. I was going to need some help with this, as I couldn't do this all on my own. But I had already tried that. I asked Mr. Poli and he turned me down, saying that I shouldn't worry about it. But looking at this, I think I did need to worry about it. Who else in the school could I go to that would help me? I could go to Mrs. Hearther. But what if she told Mr. Poli, and then I got in trouble for asking around. It had to be someone inconspicuous, someone that could go unnoticed. Someone who I could truly count on, who wouldn't betray me. And I had the perfect two people in mind. I picked up the books, and put them in the return section. I checked out the book about emotions, and walked out into the morning sun. As I headed up to my room, I thought about how I was going to approach them. Once I told them what was happening, they couldn't turn me down. They would have to listen. We could help him together.

I crept outside the dorm rooms, into the fresh morning air. Walking across the tiles of the courtyard, I tried to be as quiet as possible. I went to stand in the far corner and leaned up against the wall, waiting. I stood there for a few minutes, and checked my watch; it read 7:30. A few people came into the courtyard, and I tried to hide myself in my sweatshirt. After a few more minutes, I saw Amanda round the corner of the building into the courtyard. She went to stand in the corner opposite of me. She looked up and saw me. I motioned for her to come over to me, but she quickly looked back to the ground, averting my eyes. I tried to signal to her again, but she didn't look up. A few more students came into the courtyard. If I wanted to approach her, I would have to do it now, while not a lot of people were around. I inched along the walls, trying not to get noticed, and eventually made it over to Amanda. I tapped her on the shoulder, and she jumped, surprised to see me.

"What are you doing?" she asked in a hushed voice. "I thought I told you that we can't be friends."

"I know, I know," I said quickly. "But I really need one now. I need your help with something. You and Rohan. I can't go to anybody else about it, and you guys are the only ones that I can trust. Also, you were more than willing to be my friend back on the train. What changed?"

"One of the other kids approached us on our first day here," she sighed, relenting. "They said that we can't hang out with you. We are peasants, and you're like royalty. I don't want to be a peasant. I can't do anything about it." She looked down and wiped her face, trying to hold back tears.

"It's okay," I replied, trying to comfort her. "What if we meet in secret? We can make a time between the three of us when we don't have classes and then meet in my room. We can have a secret knock and everything!" I exclaimed, excited.

"Shh!" Amanda whispered. She looked around at the courtyard, and I did too, to see if anybody heard us. Everybody seemed to be preoccupied by something else.

"Do you really think that would work?" Amanda asked, looking up, hope in her eyes.

"I do," I replied confidently. "I am going to walk away, but when Rohan comes out, tell him the plan. Meet here in this corner early tomorrow morning, and we will talk then." I started to walk away, but Amanda grabbed my shoulder, holding me back.

"I'm sorry," she said. "About Harold and Bruce. I should have stood up for you, but I was just too scared." She looked down, ashamed.

"Hey, it's okay. You were scared about what would happen to you. Perfectly reasonable. I don't blame you for anything." I gave her a smile, trying to comfort her. Maybe I was trying to comfort myself a little too. I walked away, back to my corner. Amanda stayed in her area, and I watched as Rohan walked out of the dorms and to Amanda. I could see them whispering about something. I was assuming it was about us meeting. This will work. It had to. Now, all we had to do was wait.

I woke up early the next morning to head downstairs to meet up with Amanda and Rohan. I went to the same corner in which I had talked to Amanda the day before. Nobody else was there yet, so I just waited. A minute turned into two, which turned into ten, and still no Amanda or Rohan. Why did I give my hopes up? I thought they genuinely liked the plan. I was about to head inside back to my room, when I saw Amanda and Rohan round the corner. Once they were closer, I greeted them in a whisper.

"You came," I said, smiling from ear to ear.

"It was hard for Amanda to convince me, but if I'm being honest, I like the plan. I also need another friend," Rohan replied honestly. "We just have to be sneaky about it. And I am telling you this now: If somebody catches us, we are done. I don't want anybody to know that we are meeting with you. We'll be the laughing stock of the school, an upper, middle, and lower class citizen as friends."

"I understand," I replied. "So, when do you finish your classes?"

"My last class ends at four," said Rohan.

"Same," replied Amanda

"Ditto. So, it sounds like we can meet after class in my room. Does that work for both of you?" I asked them.

"Yes," they both replied, nodding.

"Great. I need to tell you both something, but I'll wait until tonight. Wait about ten minutes until after class ends, and when you come, just knock on the door. Why don't we just do two knocks, then one, and then two. Like this." I knocked on the stone wall twice, waited, then once, waited, then twice. "If I hear that, I'll know that it's you."

"Sounds good," said Amanda. "Meet you then."

"See you then," I replied.

After my class for the day, I hurried back to my room, and waited. After about ten minutes, just like what I said, I heard a knock at the door. Knock knock. Knock. Knock knock. I opened the door, and saw Amanda and Rohan wearing hoods over their heads, trying not to be seen. I motioned them inside, and I closed the door behind me, looking around to see if anybody was watching.

"Alright. What is it you wanted to talk to us about?" Rohan asked, as I locked the door behind me. He was shaking, as if nervous he was going to get caught. I motioned toward the bed so they could sit down. As they made their way toward the bed, they looked the room up and down, inspecting every inch of it, mouths open. Rohan sighed, closing his eyes, and Amanda put her hand on his shoulder. What was that about? Trying to forget about it, I closed the blinds, so nobody could peek into the room from the courtyard. I stood in front of them, as if giving a presentation to a class.

"I think something is wrong with my brother," I said. I filled them in on everything that had happened, from my conversation with Roger, to what I told Mr. Poli, to the book that I found in the library. Once I was finished, I took a breath, and waited for them to say something.

"Well," said Amanda, taking a breath, eyes wide, "That is a lot to take in. Do you really think whatever this 'monster' is is taking control of Roger?"

"Yes," I replied, nodding. "And I think that Mr. Poli isn't telling the whole truth. I think he knows something, but is afraid to say anything. He said that he was going to tell the other teachers about it, but I don't know if he will. And I can't go asking the teachers myself, because if I do, they might ask Mr. Poli, and then he would know that I am asking questions."

"So we just need to figure out what is happening to Roger, and we can stop it," said Rohan sarcastically. "Easy, no problemo. May I remind you that we are only three kids who just got here. Three kids who barely know how to use their magic, and we're just going to face off probably one of the most powerful beings in existence. This won't end well."

"Well we have something that this thing doesn't," I replied, excitedly. "Our magic. It may only be able to control one type of magic, or maybe none at all. If we use all three of ours, we have a chance at stopping it. We just have to figure out how to get started. Let's start with what you guys are learning in your classes."

"We're learning about how to put together different kinds of machines, and how they work. We haven't gotten to the magic part of it yet," said Rohan, sadly.

"We're learning about the stars and different constellations. But Ms. Wesmirth is also teaching us about different beasts and monsters from our myths and legends." Amanda's voice started rising in excitement. We had to shush her, just to make sure nobody heard her. "Sorry, but you just had me thinking. Maybe the beast isn't a myth. If I learn about anything that sounds like that, I can tell you guys."

"That sounds great," I said. "Mr. Poli is teaching us about mind links, and controlling other people with it."

"Well then that's it!" Rohan exclaimed. He looked toward Amanda and me, but she wore the same face of confusion as me. "You can use your mind link to force him to tell us what is wrong with him. You can also force him to not tell anybody about what we are doing. Once we figure that out, well, I don't know, but at least we will be one step closer to helping him."

"Yes!" I exclaimed. I tried to hold in my excitement, but I couldn't. I collected myself before saying anything else. "This could actually work," I said, smiling.

CHAPTER NINE

A FTER A FEW DAYS OF WAITING, WE HAD NOTHING. I WAS STARTING to doubt that we would actually be able to pull this off. Amanda still hadn't learned anything from Ms. Wesmirth, and we didn't want to try to use my mind link until she found something. If there was no evidence against him, we didn't want to confront him. The only good thing that came out of this was our secret meetings. Every afternoon, after my class, we would all meet in my room, and just talk. It was nice to be able to talk to other people my age, people who I could actually call friends. We were sitting in my room, Rohan on the floor, and Amanda and I on the bed, when Rohan came out with a bold statement.

"Why don't you just see if you could command him to do something now? I mean, it's already been a couple of days and Amanda still hasn't heard anything. And I'm tired of just waiting around. If what you say is true, and we are in danger, then we need to do something now. We can't just sit on our butts and do nothing!"

"Well remember," I said, trying to reason with him, "If we have no evidence against him, then we can't make any accusations. And plus, what good will it do to tell him to spin in a circle three times? It's not like it could help us any."

"Yes, but it will be progress. Are you once again forgetting that we have nothing? Maybe if you go in his head, you can find out at least something."

"But if you do that, wouldn't he know that Jeremy is in his head?" asked Amanda. She had a point. I had never thought of that before. If I went in his mind, he would know that I was there. And there was sure to be a rule against going into other students' heads without their permission.

"But at least it is something!" screamed Rohan.

"Lower your voice!" I yelled in a whisper, starting to get a little upset that Rohan was still pushing this idea forward. "Remember, nobody can know about this. Also, you've really been on edge lately. You good?"

"I'm fine," he replied quickly.

"You know, I can tell if you're lying. I can go into your head and figure out what is wrong if you won't tell us." I replied, a little smugly. I softened my voice. "As our friend, it is your duty to tell us if something is wrong. Right Amanda?"

"Yeah. Tell us what's wrong. We're here for you," said Amanda. She put her hand on his shoulder, and smiled at him.

"You guys wouldn't believe me if I told you," he said, looking down. Rohan started fidgeting with his fingers, eyes darting around the room, presumably trying to find something else to talk about.

"Try us," I replied optimistically, trying to coax him out of his shell. "A few weeks ago, I was just a kid locked up in my house, without any friends. Now, I talk about going into people's minds and reading their thoughts like it's nothing. And I have you guys." I smiled. Rohan looked around the room at us. We gave him encouraging smiles.

"Alright, here goes," he said, sighing. We both looked at him expectantly. "I'm not actually alive." What? Well I definitely wasn't expecting that. What was that supposed to mean? I scrunched my face in confusion, trying to convey how confused I was.

"Please elaborate," I said.

"Yes, please do," replied Amanda.

"I was killed, but somehow, I am still alive," he said. "I think it has something to do with this." He pulled up the sleeve of his jacket, revealing a bracelet, with a single charm on it: an infinity loop.

"A couple of years ago, I was walking to church with my mom. I know what you are thinking; lower-class citizens don't go to Church. And you're right. But the thing is, I wasn't lower-class, but rather, upper. My real name isn't Rohan. My real name is Gabriel Waile. I was born and raised in the upper class, but something happened where I had to make my way into the lower class. But we'll get there eventually. Anyway, I had been hearing voices in my head. I had tried to ignore them, but I couldn't. I had been sleep deprived because of it, and I slept in, almost missing Church. My mom wasn't too happy about that. And to make matters worse, while we were walking, it started to rain. Hard. We started to run, and eventually, we burst through the front doors, everybody looking up from their prayers to stare at us. I wiped down my clothes, and my mom rang out her hair, making water pour out. She looked down at me as she was doing this, and shook her head as if blaming everything on me. That was probably the last memory I have with her. A disappointment." Rohan sighed and closed his eyes. Amanda and I looked at each other, and were about to go comfort him, when he suddenly opened his eyes again. We sat back down, and Rohan continued his story.

"After a few seconds of drying off, we walked down the center aisle, getting weird looks from everybody there, and finally found a seat. We sat down, soaking the bench. We sat and participated in our normal prayers, and after a couple of minutes, a strange woman approached me. She sat down next to me and handed me this bracelet." He held up his hand, signaling to the bracelet.

"For some reason, I can't take it off. It is like it is stuck to my hand. Anyway, back to the story. At first, I didn't take it. I was skeptical of it. Why was this random lady giving me a bracelet? Should I take it? I decided to accept it, after all, what was the worst that could happen? And then she said the strangest thing. 'You will need this. You will do great things, Gabriel.' I wanted to ask her how she knew my name, but before I could, she got up and walked away. I figured I could talk to her after Church, but little did I know, I wouldn't be there after Church.

"I returned to my prayers, and services continued as normal, until we heard a scream, and a crash on the ground. It was coming from outside the Church doors. We all looked back, and suddenly, the doors swung open, revealing a little girl, probably about nine years old, blood dripping from a sharp meat knife in her hands." I suppressed a gasp and shimmied into a more comfortable position. Amanda grabbed one of the pillows and hugged it closely. I was starting to think that maybe this was as bad as he had been portraying it. Rohan, rather Gabriel, continued the story.

"But there was something strange about the girl. Her eyes were whited over, like she wasn't fully there. Her movements were also very machine-like, almost as if somebody was controlling her. Anyway, we started to run away. We all backed up against the far wall, putting as much distance between us and the girl as possible. The little girl slowly walked toward us, eying the crowd, as if looking for someone in particular. Then her eyes stopped on me. She walked slowly toward me, and I looked up toward my mom, who wore the same look of terror as me. The little girl reached me, and I ducked away, shielding my eyes. I didn't want to see what was about to happen to me." He stopped talking, sitting still. He started shivering, as he was scaring himself, even though he already knew the outcome.

"Then...she shot out...she...well...she...extending her arm...the girl...she stabbed me," he finally said. He pulled up his shirt, revealing his bony body, with a long scar running along the center of his chest. I felt a shiver run up my spine.

"I remember falling to the floor, clutching my chest. My mom screamed in horror, and went down beside me. She tried to comfort me, but both of us knew I was going to die. The other people at the church just stood there, frozen in shock. I don't know what happened to the little girl. After a few seconds, everything went black. I then opened my eyes, and I was in a giant box, a coffin. I slammed on the sides, yelling at the top of my lungs, but nobody was there. I tried to push open the coffin, but found that I couldn't. I was already in the ground. I would die in a couple of minutes from suffocation. And that's when I remembered. I should be dead. Why was I not dead? But I thought that since I was going to definitely die here, there was no reason to wonder. I waited and waited and waited, but I wasn't dying. I didn't even feel dead. And then that's when I remembered what the lady said to me at the church. She said that I would need it. I pulled up my sleeve, trying to get a look at the bracelet. It was hard to see in the dark, but I could just make out two small circles. It took me a while to figure out what they were, but eventually, I realized it was an infinity symbol. This bracelet must somehow keep me alive.

"After a couple of days, I was finally able to open up the coffin. I got a mouthful of dirt, and I spit it out. I climbed my way out, and into the graveyard. I was extremely hungry and thirsty, but once again, I couldn't die. I figured I couldn't go back to my mom, since she thought I was dead. I also figured the girl would come back and try to finish what she started if she found out I was somehow alive. I had to go somewhere where I could get food and shelter, but also go unnoticed. I decided that I had to stay with the people in the lower class and change my name. After a few days of blending in, one family took me in and took care of me. I have been there ever since. I still didn't know how the bracelet has kept me alive, but one thing is very clear. I have to find who killed me, and punish them. And I think my death, and whatever is happening to your brother may be connected. That's why I wanted to help."

CHAPTER TEN

"Wow," I said, shocked. I didn't know what else to say. How were you supposed to react when one of your best friends said that he was actually dead? I just stared at him blankly, and there were a few minutes of silence, until Amanda said something.

"What makes you think that these two incidents are connected?"

"Because," said Rohan, confidently. "If they aren't connected, then I don't have anything else to go on. If they aren't connected, then I don't know what I am going to do, or how to find the thing that did this to me. I came to Mrs. Hearther's because I thought that maybe the people here could help me. But you said that you think Mr. Poli is hiding something. What if it isn't just him? What if it is the entire staff here?"

"Well hold up," I said, trying to calm him down. "Let's not jump to conclusions. For all I know, Mr. Poli just wants to keep me safe, and out of whatever this is. Let's just focus on the things that we can control. Like learning more about this thing. Amanda will keep learning things from Ms. Wesmirth, and once we find something, I will face Roger."

"Okay," said Rohan, calming down. We were about to head our separate ways for the day, when he called us back. "Still call me Rohan. Nobody knows who I really am, not even the family who took me in. Alright?"

"Okay," we both replied. Rohan and Amanda got up and left the room, checking to make sure nobody was watching. After they left, I flopped down on my bed, and thought about what I had just learned. What else was there that I didn't know?

"I got it!" yelled Amanda, running into my room, with Rohan by her side. They both looked really excited. Maybe Amanda finally found something! "Today's lessons were all about the different myths and legends corresponding with emotions. And she talked about the legend of hate!"

"Okay," I replied excitedly. "Just lower your voice. Remember, we don't want anybody to hear us."

"Oh, right," she replied, lowering her voice to a whisper. We all sat down on the bed, and waited expectantly for Amanda to say something.

"So," she started. "Ms. Wesmirth described a creature that sounded like the one you had found in that book a few weeks ago. There is a creature that infests humans and gives them the emotion of hate. It is called a Soul Stealer."

"That's great!" I exclaimed. "Did she talk about anything else?"

"Nothing more than what we already know," Amanda replied.

"Okay. So now I can face Roger," I replied confidently.

"And then we can finally put an end to this," said Rohan.

At breakfast the next morning, I found Roger, and sat a couple of tables down. I looked over and saw Amanda and Rohan watching me. We had decided that I would first go into his mind and command him to do something, like come over to me, say a specific word, and then go back to sitting down. I went back to staring at him, and tried to get into his head. I felt a buzz in the back of my head, and then said the magic words. "Come over to me, tell me the time, and then walk back to your seat." I waited for him to come over, but he didn't. I looked up at him, and he was still eating like normal, laughing with his friends, as if nothing had happened. It didn't work! I tried a second time, but again, it didn't work. I tried one more time, this time with a different command, but still it didn't work. I had failed. I looked over the dining room to Amanda and Rohan. They both wore expressions of excitement. I shook my head, expressing my disappointment. They must have realized that it didn't work because both of their expressions changed to sadness. The rest of the day, I walked around in defeat. Was I not a powerful enough psychologist? The other day I was able to do it fine with that girl. Mr. Poli had seen me do it. He had even complimented me on it. So what was wrong? I would have to tell Amanda and Rohan that we have to come up with a new plan.

"...and so I don't know why it didn't work," I finished. Amanda and Rohan looked down, upset that it hadn't worked. Then, Rohan perked his head up.

"Well you can try one more thing!" he exclaimed. "What if you try reading his mind to see if you can find anything?"

"I don't know," I replied hesitantly. I had never done anything like that before. We were still on the basics with Mr. Poli. I didn't know if I would be able to pull it off. I voiced my concerns.

"Well I believe in you," says Amanda, confidently. "You said that Mr. Poli told you that you have inborn talent. You can do this."

"You got this," Rohan put in, encouragingly.

"Okay," I replied. I take a deep breath and close my eyes. I pictured Roger in my head. Roger, my loving and fun brother. Roger, the master in zoology. Roger, the person who gets along with everybody. I felt a ringing in my ears, and winced. I let out a whimper, and I felt a hand on my shoulder. I kept my eyes closed in concentration. I let the ringing take over me, and soon, that was all that I could hear. I succumbed to it, and felt my body fall back in the bed. Suddenly, I heard another voice in my head, but it wasn't mine. It sounded like Roger, but it was muffled, like we were underwater. He was chanting something, but I couldn't quite tell what it was. But I did hear one thing clearly, two words he kept saying over and over again, like a mantra.

"The void. The void. The void. The void." Over and over again. I figured this is all I needed. We could find out what the void was later. I opened my eyes, expecting to be in my room with Amanda and Rohan. But when I opened them, all I saw was a blue fog, with Roger in the center of it. He was turned away from me, but I could still tell that it was him. I tried to suppress a gasp.

What was this place? How was I supposed to get out of here? I knew this was a bad idea! Suddenly, Roger slowly turned around. Everything looked normal, until I saw his eyes. They were jet black.

"Well hello Jeremy," he said eerily, in an echoey voice. "I was wondering when you would arrive."

CHAPTER ELEVEN

"R OGER?" I QUESTIONED. THIS DIDN'T SOUND LIKE HIM. "AM I in your mind right now?"

"In a sense, yes," replied Roger, smiling a devilish grin from ear to ear. I felt a shiver run down my spine, chilling my entire body.

"What is going on with you Roger? Tell me. We can help you!" I tried to get through to him, but it was like he was already lost.

"I am not Roger, and you are not in his mind. But I will let you figure out on your own what I am. I wouldn't want to ruin the fun," he laughed, maniacally. "Every decision that I have made, every step that I have taken has been carefully planned out. I wouldn't want three little kids ruining all of this." I held back a gasp. How did it know about Amanda and Rohan?

"Listen Jeremy," he said, slowly stepping toward me. I backed away, not wanting to get near whatever this thing was. "You stay out of my way, and nobody has to get hurt." I was too afraid to say anything, so I just nodded my head, eyes wide in fear. Of course, I wouldn't do nothing. He was my brother. We just had to be more careful about what we did. But I was not going to let it know that.

"Good," not-Roger said. Then he turned away from me, and started walking away into the fog. I was left standing there, alone and cold. I rubbed my hands against my arms, trying to warm up, but it didn't work. I looked around, trying to find a way to get out of wherever I was, but the blue haze surrounded me, trapping me. I began to get colder and colder, my body shivering, even though there was no wind. I kneeled down on the hard ground, defeated. There was no way out of here. In my efforts to help my brother, I only doomed myself. I closed my eyes, ready for death to come to me. I lay down on the floor, curling my body into a ball. I felt my heart rate begin to slow, my body shutting down. I took one last deep breath, ready for the heavens to take me.

Suddenly, I felt a warm sensation in the back of my head. The warmth flowed from my head, down my chest and through to my arms. It reached my legs, and soon it engulfed my entire body. My eyes shot open, relit with life. I looked around me and saw the blue fog start to dissipate around me. I smiled, thankful that it wasn't my time to die. After a few seconds, the fog had completely gone away, and I was back in my room with Amanda and Rohan hovering over me, worry in their eyes.

"Good! You're awake!" Amanda exclaimed, reaching over to hug me.

"What happened?" asked Rohan. "You fell back into the bed, and then you were still for a couple of minutes. Then, you started shivering and whimpering. You were shaking uncontrollably. We tried to wake you up, but nothing worked. What happened?"

"I was inside his mind, and I could only hear two words repeating themselves over and over again: the void. I thought that that had to be a clue, but when I tried to get out, I couldn't. Then I saw him, Roger, but he was different. He warned us to stop trying to figure out what is wrong. It knew about you guys too." I stopped, taking a breath. I didn't want to tell them about my near death experience. At least, not yet. "But we aren't going to quit. We just have to be more careful about what we do."

"Agreed," said Rohan, nodding. "So, what are the next steps?" They both looked at me expectantly, as if I would know the answers. Did they expect me to be the leader? I didn't know all of the answers, and I was sure not the best person in magic. What was I supposed to tell them? But then I formulated a plan.

"Amanda, you find out anything else that you can about this monster. I will go to the library, and do some research on the void. Whatever it is, it sounds pretty self-explanatory. So Roger, do you think you could build a flying machine that could get us into the void without getting hurt?"

"I'll do my best," he replied.

"And I will find out anything I can," Amanda said.

"Alright. And are you sure that you guys are up for this? You could potentially die," I said. I was still unsure if I actually wanted to do this. But then I remembered, this was for Roger. We needed to bring him back.

"Remember," said Roger, smiling, holding up his arm containing the bracelet, "I can't die."

"And if this means that much to both of you, then I'm in too," Amanda said.

"Alright," I replied. "Let's do this."

I was back in the library the next day looking for anything that I could find on "the void," but I couldn't find anything. I was looking in every section that it could possibly be in, magical locations, biomes of Tarenburg, but it wasn't here. I wanted to ask one of the teachers if they knew anything about it, but what if I got in trouble for it? I wouldn't want that to happen. But, if it could help me save Roger, I would do it. If they question why I was asking, I would just have to make up an excuse. I walked over to one of the zoologists to ask them.

"I have a question," I told them.

"What is it?" asked one of them, not even looking at me. It was like they didn't even care.

"Can you tell me what the void is?" I asked them. All of them immediately looked up from what they were doing. One of them choked on something they were drinking. They looked at me wide-eyed. Was this a mistake? Should I not have asked about it?

"Where did you learn about the void?" the same zoologist asked, slowly.

"Oh," I replied, trying to think of an excuse. "I just saw it in a book, but it didn't explain what it was. Could you?" He looked around to make sure nobody was around to hear him, and then leaned in closer to whisper in my ear.

"The void is a place out the back of the twenty-year-olds' building. It is literally a giant void. Nobody knows how it got there, or how deep it is. All of the teachers warn us not to go near there, in fear that we may fall down. You're not thinking of going there, are you?" he asked skeptically.

"No!" I replied quickly. "I would never even think about it. That sounds really scary." I tried to sound as convincing as I could. And I wasn't telling a whole lie. It did sound really scary. "Thanks," I said, walking away. Now I just had to tell Amanda and Rohan.

Later that day, in my room, I told Amanda and Rohan what I learned.

"That's good," Rohan said. "I will need a few more days, maybe a week to finish the machine. Is it okay if I build it in here? That way, I can work on it with you guys too, if you have any ideas."

"I'm not so sure that that would be a good idea," I said. "We don't know how big it would be, and it would probably make too much noise and wake everybody else up. We need to find a big place that is far away from everybody so nobody finds out what we are doing."

"Well then what do you suggest we do?" Amanda asked. "Just build it right in the middle of the courtyard? In the field? Everybody would see it!"

"We need to find a place where nobody would find us, and is big enough to fit the machine until we use it," Rohan said, scrunching his face, seemingly trying to think of the perfect place. Where would be the perfect place? The only huge place that would work would be the courtyard, but that was too exposed. So are the field and dining hall. We couldn't use the classrooms because we didn't want the teachers knowing what we were doing. The only other place that was big enough to house the machine was...wait. Could it work?

"I have an idea," I said. Amanda and Rohan looked up at me, their eyes telling me to go on. "But I think it would be better if I showed you."

"How did you find this place?" Amanda asked in awe, looking up at the pillars of the cavern under the courtyard.

"I was just exploring and I happened to stumble across it," I replied.

"What do you think this was for? Does Mrs. Hearther know about this?" asked Rohan.

"I was questioning the same thing," I replied. "I'm still in awe of it myself."

"This would definitely work," Rohan said. "Now all we need is supplies."

"Yeah. And Ms. Wesmirth said that she would give us some books on the beasts related to emotions," Amanda added. "I could ask if I could get any extras on the Soul Stealer."

"Okay," I said. "Let's do this."

CHAPTER TWELVE

THE NEXT DAY, I DECIDED TO SNEAK IN A LITTLE EARLY, AND AFTER a few minutes, Amanda and Rohan walked in, carrying what looked like parts to a machine. There were wires, screws, metal plates, and some things that I had never seen before. I couldn't keep up with it all! They walked toward the center of the cavern, and tried to place them all down softly, failing in the process, making loud clanging noises reverberating off of the walls.

"That's a lot of stuff," I observed.

"Oh really. You don't say," said Rohan, sarcastically, out of breath. Both of them fell to the floor, breathing hard.

"Do you guys need water or anything?" I asked slowly. "You know I could have helped. How did you even get that all in here without anybody noticing?"

"We're fine. We just waited until most people were inside and slunk along the edges. Not many people take much attention to lower- and middle-class kids," said Amanda, starting to stand up. She wobbled a little, and decided to sit back down.

"Just a quick question," I said. "How big is this going to be? Are we going to be able to fit it through the cave exit?" Rohan looked at the machine, and it looked like he did some calculations in his head. His eyes moved back and forth, as if looking at an invisible chalkboard, full of equations.

"It should," he finally said, nodding his head. "Some of the supplies here we might not even need. And we might need some more supplies if we want all of us to fit in there."

"About that," I said slowly. I had been thinking a lot about all of us going into the void together. "I am not sure we should all go in. I think I should just go in, without you guys." They started to argue with me, but I put up my hands, quieting them. "This thing is really dangerous, and it already knows about you guys. I won't have you getting hurt for this."

"But how am I supposed to control the machine if I'm not there?" asked Rohan.

"I was thinking about that, and I think I have a solution. If I can use my mind link to hear other people's thoughts, then surely, I can use it to connect what we see."

"Are you sure that you could actually do this?" asked Amanda. "I mean, nobody has ever even done that before. How do you know that that's actually possible?"

"Come on," I said. "We can literally control plants, people, animals, and machines with our minds! We can teleport anywhere in the world with just a thought! A few weeks ago, none of us thought that that was real. Just because somebody has never done it before, doesn't mean it can't be done. Just think about the first person who tried magic. Other people probably laughed at them before they actually did it. It all just starts with an idea."

"Well that's all handy dandy and inspirational and all, but we still need to test if it works. Why don't you try it now on Amanda while I start to put together this machine," Rohan said, walking over to the pile of machine parts on the floor.

"Okay," I said. "This should be easy. It's just the same concept as going into their minds, just this time, what they see." I stared into her eyes, and did the same procedure that I would do if I were going to go into somebody's head, except instead of focusing on their mind, I focused on their eyes. After a few minutes, I started to hear a buzzing sound, but instead of feeling it in the back of my head, it was in my eyes. Amanda reached toward her eyes, and started to squeeze them.

"Succumb to the ringing, Amanda," I said. We took deep breaths, and closed our eyes. After a few seconds, the ringing went away, and I opened my eyes. Amanda opened hers too and I noticed that her eyes are glowing. I ran to the river to see my reflection and saw that mine were too. Rohan dropped his tools, and looked up at us in awe. Suddenly, my view changed, and I wasn't looking at the mirror anymore. Rather, I was looking down at a pair of hands, but they weren't mine. They were too small to be me, and they weren't my skin color. I was looking through Amanda's eyes! This was amazing.

"This is so cool," I whispered. Amanda's head looked up toward my body and I saw myself. I was frozen in the position that I was in while looking at myself in the water. I was about to say something else, but I felt the stinging near my eyes again, and I succumbed to it. After a few seconds, my view changed again, and I was in my own body. I turned around to look at Amanda and Rohan. Rohan was looking at us in amazement. Amanda looked a little woozy, so I walked her to the bed.

"That," she whispered, "Was awesome!"

"What did you see?" I asked Amanda.

"I just saw you and your eyes were glowing. You weren't moving. I felt a tingling sensation in my eyes. Was that you?" she asked.

"Yeah it was," I replied. "I was seeing things through you. Now, we just have to figure out a way to reverse it, so you can see what I see."

"Do you know how to do that?" Amanda asked.

"I'm not sure. Do you have any ideas?" I asked Rohan. We both turned to look at him, but he was still frozen in shock, mouth wide forming an O. "Rohan?" I walked over to him and waved my arms in front of his face. He didn't even blink.

"Ugh. Let me handle this," Amanda said, walking over to him. She stood in front of him, and promptly smacked him across the face.

"Ouch!" Rohan screamed, rubbing the side of his face where Amanda hit him. I tried to suppress a laugh, and managed to only let out a little giggle. "That was amazing! Both of your eyes started glowing! I have never seen anything like it before!"

"So I guess it is possible," I said. "Do you have any ideas of how we could get it to where it is reversed, where Amanda can see what I see, and I can normally function?"

"I have no idea," he said, shaking his head, still in awe. "I'm still just surprised that that actually worked. I don't think that that has ever happened before. You guys just changed psychology for the better. I mean, if you can do that, what's to say you can't feel the same things as others, or taste the same things as others. Maybe you can, like, project your spirit out of your body so your physical body can be stationary in one place, but your consciousness can go somewhere else. Imagine all of the possibilities!" His eyes widened with wonder. But he was right. If we could connect what we see, what was stopping us from doing all of the things that Rohan mentioned. Before, when I left home, it was only a dream that we could change the world. Now, we might actually be able to do that.

Chapter Thirteen

For the next couple of days, Amanda and I had been working to perfect the eye-to-eye connection. It took a while, but we were able to figure out how to reverse it. Rohan was almost done with the machine. He said that it should be done today. The three of us snuck into the cavern, and Rohan immediately walked toward the machine. The room had turned into a jungle gym of notes, machine parts, and the machine itself. Amanda and I sat down and practiced the mind link for the last time.

"You ready?" I asked her.

"You bet," she replied. I concentrated on Amanda, and almost immediately, our eyes started to glow. I closed my eyes, and let the ringing take over my body. Then, I felt another force in the back of my eyes: Amanda. I looked up, and saw her body, still as stone on the floor, eyes still glowing. After a couple of minutes, the ringing returned, our eyes stopped glowing, and everything returned to normal.

"I was thinking," Rohan said, still tinkering with the machine. "Seeing through our eyes is great and all, but it won't do any good if we can't talk to each other. We should also practice going into your eyes, and head at the same time."

"That's a good idea," I replied, nodding my head. "Amanda, I will go into your head, and once I am there, we will be able to talk to each other through my mind link. Then, we will do the same thing we have been doing for the past couple of days."

"But what if I get stuck?" she asked, scared.

"Don't worry. Everything will be okay," I said reassuring her. I wasn't just saying it for her, but also for me. "I think the reason it was different was because the beast wasn't human. I have been practicing with Mr. Poli, and that has never happened. It is going to be okay."

"Okay," she said. "Let's do it." I closed my eyes, and pictured Amanda in my head. I went through the same procedure that I had done many times earlier. I heard a ringing in the back of my mind, and I let it take over me. After a couple of seconds, I could not only hear my voice in my head, but also Amanda's.

"Alright," I thought. "Can you hear me?"

"Yes," replied Amanda. I sighed in relief. I was afraid that it wouldn't have worked. We moved on to the next part, and performed it like second nature. Our eyes started glowing, and I felt a tingling sensation in the back of my eyes. After a few seconds, it went away.

"It worked!" Amanda exclaimed in my head. I could feel all of her excitement come over me like a wave.

"Great!" I said back. "We should probably keep it going for a couple more minutes, just to get in the practice."

"Agreed." We did this for a couple of minutes, Amanda and I talking, and Rohan working on the machine. After a while, Amanda and I separated from each other.

"That was amazing!" she said, out loud.

"I know!" I replied excitedly. It really was possible! "How much longer do you think you need with the machine?" I asked Rohan.

"This is the last screw," he said, grinding his teeth. He was turning a screw tightly into place. Once he was finished with that, he got up and wiped the sweat off of his face with his sleeve. "So all you have to do is sit here," he said, pointing to a makeshift seat in the middle of the machine. "And then once we use the mind link, I will be able to control it. Just a quick question before we go, though. Do we know what we are looking for?"

"Well, not exactly," I said slowly. "But any clue that may be able to help us find Roger. Maybe there is a bottom to the pit, and he is down there, and we just need to bring him back up."

"And what if we don't find anything?" asked Amanda.

"We have to. Or else, this was all for nothing," I said, trying to convince myself, more than them. "Tomorrow afternoon, we will meet here in my room like normal. But after lights out, we will sneak out and go to the void. This will work."

The next day, I could barely focus on anything but the void. This was it. This was the day that we were going to save Roger. I waited in anticipation the whole day, until finally my psychology class was over, and I rushed to the secret passage. Amanda and Rohan were already waiting for me.

"Hey guys," I said, stepping on the pressure plates, opening the staircase.

"Hey. I just realized something," said Rohan. This didn't sound good.

"What?" I asked, scared. This might ruin our entire plan. What if it won't work?

"You were able to do your mind link with Amanda with no problem, but you were never able to do it with two people before. Are you sure that you can do that?" Oh no! In our haste to figure out how to connect our eyes and mind with Amanda, I had completely forgotten that I also had to use my mind link with Rohan! This could ruin our entire plan.

"Well we don't know until we try," I said, trying to sound more confident than I was. Once we reached the bottom, we all formed a circle, and I focused on Amanda. I was able to do it with her without any issues, since we had done it many times before. Now was the tricky part. I tried to do the same thing that I had been doing with Amanda. I focused on him, and I heard a ringing in the back of my head.

"Do you hear a ringing?' I asked Rohan.

"Yes," he replied, sounding a little scared.

"It's okay. It is nothing to be afraid of. Let it take over you." After a couple of seconds, it had fully surrounded me, and I let it take control of me.

"Hello?" I asked in my head.

"I'm here," replied Amanda. "Are you here Rohan?" We waited a couple of seconds, and there was no response. Of course this wouldn't work. Why did I give my hopes up.

"Don't give up yet," said Amanda, in my head.

"How did you know that I was thinking about giving up?" I ask.

"Well, I can read your thoughts, remember?"

"Right," I replied, feeling silly I had forgotten that. After a few seconds, I heard a small voice in the back of my head.

"I'm here," Rohan said weakly.

"It's okay. It's not going to hurt you. I know you are scared right now. That is how I felt the first time it happened to me too, but it is okay," I said, reassuring him. It worked!

"Okay," he said quietly in my head. "Okay," he said a little bit louder. He said it over and over again, until both Amanda and I could hear him loud and clear.

"You did it!" I exclaimed in my head. "And it worked!"

"Well we don't know for sure yet," said Rohan. "We still don't know if I can get inside of your head yet."

"Alright," I replied, now full of confidence. "Let's try it." We did the same thing, and I felt a tingling in my eyes, I looked up at Rohan, and I saw that his eyes were glowing, meaning it was working. I let the ringing wash over me, and then it went away.

"Is it working?" I asked Rohan.

"It is! This is so cool!" exclaimed Rohan. "Is it still working for you, Amanda?"

"It is!" she responded, happiness in her voice.

"Okay. One more test," I said, getting more and more excited by the second. "We have to see if you can control the machine while you are in my head."

"Oh, yeah! I almost forgot," Rohan said, sheepishly. "Let me try." For a few seconds, nothing happened. I could hear Rohan's concentrated pants, but the machine still didn't move.

"You got this," Amanda said, encouragingly. After a few more seconds, the machine was still stationary in the same place it had been when Rohan finished working on it. I was about to give up, when I heard a whirring sound coming from Rohan's machine. One of the motors was turning!

"It's working!" he exclaimed, proudly. It was like a miracle! Everything was going according to plan. All we had to do was go into the void and find Roger. How hard could that be?

CHAPTER FOURTEEN

"THIS IS HARDER THAN I THOUGHT IT WOULD BE," ROHAN SAID, grunting, trying to move the machine. Amanda and I were supporting Rohan by holding the machine from below.

"How much does this thing weigh?" I asked.

"You think I know?" asked Rohan, putting the machine down and letting out a huge sigh of relief. "I didn't think it was going to be this heavy. I'm just surprised nobody has heard us!"

"Come on guys. We almost have it," Amanda said encouragingly.

"Yeah. Just a couple more minutes of moving this machine. No biggie." Rohan said, exasperated.

"You okay?" I asked Rohan.

"Yeah. Let's do this." Rohan looked at the machine, face grimacing in concentration. After a few seconds, some of the motors started to turn, and in a couple of places, some steam escaped. Rohan let the motors run for a couple of seconds, and then lifted the machine off of the ground again. It sputtered for a little, and I was afraid that it might fall down, but Rohan got it under control, and steered it back on course. He slowly but surely guided it toward the exit.

After a while, many grunts, and almost mishaps, passing pillar after pillar, we reached the exit. Rohan set down the machine and fell down onto the grass, lying down.

"Great job!" Amanda exclaimed. She went over and gave him a giant hug.

"That was amazing," I added. "Do you need to stop for a break?"

"No, I got this. The journey isn't over yet," he replied. He took a deep breath, and stood back up. He got the machine working again, and we slowly moved out of the forest and into the clearing, where we crossed the field where Mrs. Hearther demonstrated her magic the first day we got there. I had taken a map of the school from the library, so I knew the way. We crept across the lawn, trying to make as little noise as possible. We walked along the side of the building, feet squelching in the grass, trying to keep in the shadows. Once we were free of the building, we started walking faster toward the twenty-year-olds' building. We finally saw it in the distance, and then made a left, toward the void. It was just like that zoologist had said in the library. It was a literal void in the middle of the ground, leading to nowhere. Rohan set down the machine, letting out a giant breath, as if he had been holding it the entire time. He lay down in the grass to rested for a little. I crept over toward the edge of the void and looked down. There was a white mist on the bottom, like clouds. I couldn't see the bottom. We took a couple of seconds to rest, and then went over the plan.

"Are you sure you want to do this?" asked Amanda.

"Don't talk me out of it now," I replied, trying to laugh it off. Then I got serious. "This is my brother. I need to save him, no matter what it takes."

"Okay," she said. I climbed up the machine, and into the seat.

"You won't need to do anything, but look around," Rohan said, as he circled his machine, checking it one last time. "Amanda will be your second set of eyes in case you miss anything, and I will be controlling the machine. Are you ready?"

"As ready as I'll ever be," I replied, a little scared. I connected our minds and eyes, and in a couple of minutes, we were ready.

"Okay. Let's do this," Rohan said in my head. He concentrated on the machine, and I could tell that this was harder than usual for him. We had never tried doing it with me in the seat. Eventually, we made it off the ground, and the machine moved over the void. It was wobbly at first, and I could tell that this was taking all of Rohan's concentration. He straightened it out, and then slowly started to descend.

"Are you doing okay?" asked Amanda in my head.

"I'm alright," I thought back. It wasn't me I was worried about, but Rohan. This used all of his concentration, and if he lost it for even a second, then I was done for. I just hoped that he could do it.

"I can," Rohan said in my head. He must have heard my thoughts! "Yes, I can hear your thoughts. Remember, our minds are connected. Now try to be quiet and just look for anything that can help us." I looked up and around me, but I couldn't see anything yet. The opening of the void was getting farther and farther away from me, and the fog closer. But still, there was nothing.

"Can you see anything, Amanda?" I asked.

"Nothing yet," she replied. We kept going further down. The mist was getting closer, and if I reached out my hands, I could touch it. We dived into the depths of the fog, and after a few seconds, I could barely see anything. I couldn't tell which way was up or down, left or right. I started to panic. If I couldn't see anything, then neither could they.

"Are you okay?" I asked Rohan.

"I can't see anything," he replied.

"Neither can I," said Amanda. "Do you want to come up now?"

"No," I replied. "If we go up now, we might as well give up. And I am not giving up, unless we absolutely have to. We are going to find him."

"I don't know how much longer I can go," Rohan said sadly. "If I can't see anything, I won't know if there is anything in the way for me to avoid. And if we go too far down, we may lose our sense of direction completely. And then we won't be able to get out at all."

"Rohan is right," Amanda said in my head. "We better turn back now if we want to fight another day." But I couldn't give up. Not now.

"Don't think of it as giving up," Amanda said reassuringly. "Think of it as temporarily retreating to gather more information. Maybe we can find another way to traverse the void or a special tool that we can use to see through the fog." I knew she was right, but I didn't want to admit it to myself. But I guess we didn't have another choice. We had to go back up. I started to feel the machine move in an upward direction. After a little, I broke through the fog, and could see the top of the void. I looked out and saw the still faces of Amanda and Rohan, eyes glowing. Even though they had no facial expressions, I could still tell that they were disappointed. We failed.

CHAPTER FIFTEEN

I SPENT THE NEXT DAY WALKING AROUND CAMPUS IN A HAZE OF SADNESS. I couldn't stop thinking about our failure last night. After everything, we had moved the machine back into the cavern via the cave entrance and swore to never touch it again. Everything had been going to plan! The machine worked, the mind links worked, but it was all for nothing. Usually I was excited for Mr. Poli's class, but today I walked in, slumped over, defeated. I didn't want anything to do with psychology. It was a sign of my failure. How could I save Roger? There was no way to do it! I sat down in my usual spot, and listened to Mr. Poli drone on about proper technique mumbo jumbo. I could hardly stay focused. I was about to fall asleep when Mr. Poli said something interesting.

"You know, there is this place I have always wanted to visit," he said, with a sparkle in his eyes, like a kid looking at a treat after dinner. "There is a legend that talks about a place called the Psyche Tree. It is where psychologists' powers are enhanced to do great things. Legends say that a group of practitioners long ago went there and started the idea of God throughout mankind, and so the Church was born."

"Well," I said, trying to start a conversation, now intrigued. "If that is true, then magic isn't just a small line between science and the church. It means that magic is the church. Our entire religion is based on what some psychologists thought up thousands of years ago. Are you saying that the church is a lie?"

"Well personally, I never believed any of that. It is all just lies fed to us by our leaders," he replied.

"But it's not their fault then!" I exclaimed, trying to come to their defense. "It isn't their fault that they believe that! And how do you know that what the church says isn't real? What if those practitioners found proof of divinity, and wanted to let everybody know about it?"

"Well, believe what you want to, I still think it is all lies."

"Well then you're wrong," I said under my breath. If it was all fake, then my entire upbringing was a lie. I was raised on believing in the Church. But now, I didn't know. And then I remembered back to the day that I arrived at Mrs. Hearther's. Dad had just disappeared, kind of like what happened with Ms. Wesmirth. If he was practicing magic, and he knew that magic was real, then why was he the pastor of the church? Unless it was all an act? I wanted to think about it more, but something else was pulling at my mind. I felt like there was something else that I should be taking away from this conversation. And then an idea started to sprout in my mind.

After class, I ran to the cavern, expecting to see Amanda and Rohan, but they weren't there. I waited for a while and checked my watch. It said it was 5:00, but they still weren't here. I waited a little bit longer, and that little bit longer turned into ten minutes, which turned into twenty. They weren't coming. It was probably because of our failure yesterday. But they had said to think about this like a minor setback, not a full out dismissal of the plan. And I had something important to tell them! Should I go to the dorms and knock on their door? I would risk getting caught. But I had to! If not for me, then also for Rohan. This was as much of a personal vendetta for him as it was for me. I made my way toward the exit and back to the entrance of the school. Creeping along the edges of the building, I tried not to catch the glance of the few guards stationed in towers above the entrance. After slinking past them, I walked across the courtyard, to the dorm building, and counted the doors leading to Amanda's room. I did our secret knock, two long, one short, and then two long again.

"What do you want?" asked Amanda.

"Can I come inside?" I asked.

"Sure," she replied glumly. I heard the lock click, and then the door cracked open and I rushed inside. I took the time to look around Amanda's room. It was nothing like mine. The walls were torn and there was dirt and grime in every corner. The bed had a blanket so thin, you might as well not even use it. The bathroom was even dirtier than the walls, with mold congregating everywhere you looked, and a shower head that wasn't screwed completely to the wall. I looked over at Amanda, and immediately started feeling bad for her. I imagined Rohan's room was the same, if not worse. This wasn't how anybody should be treated! I just stood there in shock and after a couple of seconds, told her my plan.

"So," I started, "Mr. Poli was teaching us today and he mentioned a tree called the Psyche Tree. It is a tree where phycologists' powers are enhanced. What if we go there, and I can try to use my mind link to get to the real Roger?"

"And how do you know that this will work?" she asked. "I mean, everything went right when we were preparing to go into the void. Then when we actually tried it, it didn't work. What's to say that this time won't be the same?"

"I don't know," I replied truthfully. "But last night, you said to think about this as a minor setback. Why are you so down in the dumps about it now?"

"Well, I was thinking about it today, and I don't know what else we could do! That was the only thing we had to go off of, and now that lead is gone."

"But what about my idea?"

"Jeremy, you can't think about life as an optimist," she said, putting her hands on my shoulders. "It won't work. You have to live as a realist."

"But what if it does work!" I exclaimed. "You're right. Maybe this plan doesn't work. But we at least have to try. I am going to get Rohan and tell him the plan."

"Whatever," said Amanda. I went out her door, and knocked on Rohan's. He opened it, got one look at me, and immediately tried to close it again, but I was faster and put my foot in the door.

"Just listen to me," I said.

"What? What do you want?" he asked. "Our only chance of catching this monster is gone."

"I think I have another plan," I told him. "Just come over to Amanda's room, and I'll tell you everything."

"How can you have so much optimism? Literally just last night our mission that we thought was fool proof failed."

"But we have to keep on trying. I don't want my brother gone forever, and I know that you don't want to be immortal forever either."

"How do you know that?" he said.

"Because I know that when you had a plan, you would do anything for it. Also, if you're immortal, you will have to watch all of your friends die, your family die. And you would be here forever. Alone, without anyone to comfort you. Come on, let's do this!" I said, trying to encourage him.

Rohan looked down at his fingers and started fidgeting with them. After a few seconds, he took a deep breath and looked up. "Okay fine. Let's hear your big plan." I walked him over to Amanda's room, and we all filed into the cramped space that it was. I repeated the plan to Rohan.

"And do we even know where this tree is? What if it's on the other side of the world?" asked Rohan.

"Well then I guess we'll just have to take that risk. This is the only other way that I can think of to get answers. Do you have any better ideas?"

"No," he replied glumly.

"But if you ask Mr. Poli more information about it, he'll get suspicious. Is there another way to find more information about it?" asked Amanda.

"I'm sure the library has something about it. I can spend tomorrow looking for it."

"Fine," said Rohan, finally. "But if this plan doesn't work, I am giving up. I mean, you could have died when we went into the void. How do you know that this isn't as dangerous?"

"I don't," I replied truthfully. "But if there is even a slight chance that we can defeat this beast, we have to take it."

"Okay," Rohan replied.

"We'll do this," said Amanda.

The next day after breakfast, I walked through the doors of the library and was greeted with the smell of fresh books. I walked over to the section about psychology and scanned the shelves for the book I was looking for. I didn't know what it was yet, but I knew I would know it when I saw it. I came to the section about magical places and picked out a book that looked promising. Sitting down, I opened the book, and began to read. I read for a couple minutes until I finally flipped to a page that read, "The Psyche Tree." Under those words, it had a picture of a giant tree. It was taller and wider than any that I had seen before. Its branches seemed to reach all the way to the heavens, and in the middle of the tree, the branches seemed to almost bend inward and around each other to form an eye. No wonder it was called the Psyche Tree. I read down the long paragraph of words until I came to a section about its location. It said that nobody had seen it in generations, but the last person to see it left a clue as to where it was. It read:

> To reach this long forgotten place,
> Your knowledge of Tarenburg you mustn't misplace
> First, you must find the school of science and magic
> And then the field of many smells
> (Don't get trapped, it will be tragic)
> Traverse to the midpoint of these two locations
> To find the Psyche Tree, the founder of all creations
>
> But beware this trip will not be easy
> It will be scary, loud, threatening, and breezy
> Few have lived to tell the tale
> That is my warning, be safe, farewell.

Putting the bookmark in the page with the riddle, I closed the book, and then my eyes. I let out a deep breath and groaned. Why couldn't people just flat out tell you what they mean? Why was everything in riddles? Obviously the school of magic and science was Mrs. Hearther's School of the Sciences, but what was the field of many smells? I went to find a map of Tarenburg, and once I did, I tried to find this field. I located the train station connecting everything in Tarenburg and followed the train tracks to Mrs. Hearther's School of the Sciences. Once I found the school, I looked around the map to see if I could locate whatever the field of many smells was.

I sat there for most of the morning, reading under a dim light. I was about to give up when something caught my eye. There was a small area not far from Mrs. Hearther's. It was painted with all of the colors of the rainbow, from red to green, purple, and blue. If the map hadn't been so old, and the colors faded, I might have spotted it a lot easier. Tiny characters on top of it spelled out

"The Flowering Field." This had to be it! I went to the description of the different places at the bottom of the map, and once I read the description of the Flowering Field, I knew my suspicions had been true.

The Flowering Field was a small field containing all different types of flowers, oxeyes, poppies, roses, and more. No wonder the author called it the field of many smells. I looked back to the map and placed my fingers on the two locations. I brought them together, and when my fingers met each other, I picked them up to see where they intersected. I suppressed a gasp as my eyes rested on the location: The Forest Lush. Maybe the stories were true. Maybe the Forest Lush was haunted. Maybe the Psyche Tree was in the forest. I closed the book, checked it out, and headed over to my room to put the book away and show the others what I learned.

CHAPTER SIXTEEN

A MONTH GOES BY REALLY SLOWLY WHEN YOU HAVE SOMETHING you are looking forward to. When you are going to go on a big vacation, and you can start the countdown a week away, that week seems to go on forever. That is what it was like for that month after we decided that we were going to go to the Psyche Tree. While in Mr. Poli's class, I learned about the human mind, how it worked, and different ways to control it without getting lost. But in my secret meetings with Amanda and Rohan, I had been learning to perfect the skill that we made up. We liked to call it "sight seeing."

Ms. Wesmirth had been teaching Amanda a lot about the different myths and legends. We had been speculating that since the Soul Stealer wasn't a myth, then there are probably some others that weren't as well. We had been learning everything we could about them, just in case we needed it. Amanda had also almost mastered teleporting. She could teleport, but getting the correct place that she wanted to go to was hard for her.

Under Mr. Ringly's supervision, Rohan had been perfecting his engineering magic, and could now control different machines with ease. He could also control small pieces of machinery with precision. He could command a nail to hit the middle of a bullseye, and force a scrap of metal to start hurling toward something at a surprisingly fast speed. One afternoon, when Amanda and Rohan came for our daily meeting, I was ready to tell them the big news.

"Guys, I think we are ready," I told them.

"Ready for what?" asked Amanda.

"To go to the Psyche Tree! We've become so much more powerful over this past month, and I think that we are finally ready to do this!"

"But I can't teleport correctly! What if something goes wrong, and I need to get us out of there? I won't be able to do anything, and you guys will be stuck there to face whatever is there."

"But we don't even know if there is anything there to begin with! Waiting was just a safety precaution. What do you think?" I asked, turning to Rohan.

"I think we are ready," he replied, not looking up.

"How can you say that? We still need more time to practice!" Amanda insisted.

"Well then I guess we'll just have to go without you," Rohan replied indignantly.

"And you know very well that I am not going to let that happen," Amanda replied.

"Then come with us!" I insisted.

"Fine," Amanda said. "But if something goes wrong, don't say I didn't warn you. So, how are we going to do this?"

"We'll sneak out tonight, after lights out." I pulled out the map of Tarenburg, and pointed to the Forest Lush. "The forest is northwest of here, and it's not even that far away, maybe an hour walk. Then, we'll make our way through the forest, and find the Psyche Tree. Then, I will use my mind link to talk to Roger, and then we'll save him." I looked up at the two of them, and Rohan had a little smile on his face. Amanda was shaking her head.

"This isn't going to work," Amanda said under her breath.

After lights out, we crept our way downstairs and out the front door of the building. We brought nothing but a flashlight, and a few pieces of metal for Rohan to control. We made our way through the courtyard, and out the front gates of the school. I looked at the map, and figured out which way we needed to go. We stayed quiet, trying to keep to the ground as much as possible. Once we left the boundaries of the school, we got up and started walking at a normal pace.

"So we just need to keep going straight, and we will make it," I said, looking at the map. I rolled it up and put it in my pocket, careful not to crease it too much. We walked in silence for a couple of minutes, until Amanda said something.

"This is a stupid idea. We're going to die."

I sighed. "This is as much of a risk as going to the void was. Plus, you said that you would help us in any way that you could. We need to stop this beast! And besides, remember my promise? If this doesn't work, then we'll stop." We kept quiet and kept walking. The cicadas chirping in the almost pitch black added to the eeriness of the night. Finally we reached what looked like a wall of trees. But even in the darkness, I could still tell that it was different, magical. It was the Forest Lush.

"Do we really have to go inside?" asked Amanda, sounding a little scared.

"Relax. Everything will be okay," I replied.

"I hope you're right," said Amanda.

I turned to her. "Look, if you don't want to go inside, I totally understand. You can turn back now if you want. Just keep going in that direction, and you'll reach the school. We'll see you in the morning."

"No!" Amanda insisted. "I'm not letting you two boys go in there by yourself. What if something goes wrong, and we need to get out of there quickly? I'm going in there." And then without another word, she walked right into the forest, letting the trees swallow her up. We followed her in, a little more cautiously than her.

"We should link hands," said Rohan. "That way, we don't lose each other."

"Good idea," I replied, reaching out my hand to the direction of where I heard Rohan's voice. I felt his arm, and reached down to hold his hand. I felt a hand on my other shoulder, Amanda's, and I let it sit there, as I needed that hand to hold the flashlight. Even though the flashlight we brought was bright, it did us almost no good. It was like the trees swallowed all of the light. Most of the moon's light was blotted out by the trees. We walked slowly into the woods, trying to keep a lookout for anything that could jump out at us. As we moved closer and closer into the heart of the forest, the tension got higher, and higher, and higher. We started walking even slower, trying to take everything in. There was a rustle in the trees, and we heard a loud chirp reverberating throughout the forest. I pointed the flashlight upwards to where I heard the noise, but I couldn't see anything.

We kept walking, and I heard Amanda and Rohan's breathing disappear, as if they were holding it in. Everything got quiet, and soon, I couldn't even hear the grass squelching under my feet. I started to feel a chill run down my spine, even though there was no wind. Then suddenly, I heard a ringing in my head. It was more powerful than any I had ever experienced before when using my mind link. I fell to the ground, and the flashlight fell out of my hands. I let go of Rohan and put my hands to my ears. I screamed out.

"What's wrong?" asked Amanda, coming down beside me. I could hear panic in her voice.

"I don't know!" I exclaimed. "I hear a loud overbearing ringing in my ears. It's stronger and louder than any I have ever experienced before."

"The Psyche Tree," Rohan said.

"What?" asked Amanda, looking up.

"It's probably the Psyche Tree. We are probably getting closer to it. Maybe if we get closer, it will start to go away. Come on," he said, picking me up and lifting my left arm over his shoulder. Amanda did the same, but with my right arm. She held the flashlight in her other hand. I started walking, but the ringing was unbearable, and I had to close my eyes. I shook my head, trying to get the ringing out. But rather than go away, it seemed to be getting louder and louder the further we walked. I started breathing harder, and it was taking all of my willpower just to stay upright. I let out a loud scream that seemed to wake the whole forest. Through the ringing, I could hear the wing beats of different birds flying away, the branches they were just on moving back and forth making the leaves shake in a violent manner. Soon, the ringing took over me, and I couldn't hear anything but it. I let out another scream, at least, I thought I did, and fell to the ground. But as I fell, I heard the ringing noise start to dissipate, and go away. I sat up, holding my throbbing head. I looked around. The forest was gone. We were in a giant clearing, a huge circle of grass. I heard Amanda and Rohan gasp, and I felt a hand tap me on my shoulder.

"Look," I heard Amanda saying. I slowly brought my head up, and I let out a giant breath too. In the middle of the field was a giant tree, its branches twisting upwards and forming a giant eye. I let myself smile, and collapsed to the ground. We had found it! The Psyche Tree.

CHAPTER SEVENTEEN

"WOAH," I WHISPERED, LOOKING UP AT THE MONOLITH OF A tree that it was. I got off my feet and started to walk toward it. It was so tall, I couldn't see the top of it. I looked over my shoulder to Amanda and Rohan, and they both had the same expression of awe and amazement as me. It was like nothing I had ever seen before! I reached out my hand to touch its bark, and as soon as I did, it was like I could feel everybody in existence, everybody that was, is, and will be. I felt something that I had never felt before, but I couldn't quite put my finger on it.

"This has got to be, like, thousands of years old!" Rohan observed, walking the perimeter of the tree.

"It is," I replied.

"How do you know that?" asked Amanda, curious.

"Whenever I touch the tree, it is as if I can feel the consciousness of everybody that ever was and will be. The earliest consciousness I can detect is from a few thousand years ago. How do you think the tree got like this?" I questioned.

"I have no idea," replied Rohan, still observing the tree. "So what are you going to do? Meditate? Climb the tree?"

"I think that since I can feel everybody's consciousness when I touch it, I will just try to focus on Roger's and use my mind link to try to contact him."

"Okay," replied Amanda. "And we are here if you need us." Rohan went to stand next to Amanda, and they took a couple of steps back. I slowly walked toward the tree, and extended my hand out toward it. I took a deep breath, and touched the tree's ancient bark. As I did that, I used my mind link to try to connect to Roger, but before I could find him, I heard a scream behind me. It was Amanda. I spun around and let my hand let go of the tree. I saw Amanda fall down to the ground, her hands holding her head. Rohan sat down to be eye-level with her, fear in his eyes. I ran over to Amanda to try to help her. My hands fumbled in confusion and panic.

"What's wrong?" asked a panicked Rohan.

"I don't know! There's like a sharp ringing in my head, kind of like what would happen if you used your mind link on me, Jeremy!" Amanda exclaimed in between breaths. She closed her eyes again and let out another agonizing scream, waking the forest a second time that night. "It is stronger than anything I have ever felt before. Is it you?"

"No, it can't be me. My hand isn't on the tree, and why would I be using my mind link on you?" I asked, concerned. Did this have anything to do with the Psyche Tree? Maybe Amanda was right. Maybe we shouldn't have come here.

"I told you we shouldn't have come here," she said, as if reading my mind. "What is doing this?"

"I'm honestly surprised you haven't figured it out yet. I thought you kids were smarter than this," said a voice in the woods. The voice sounded familiar, but I couldn't figure out who it was.

"Who are you?" I asked, trying to sound brave. I looked around to see if I could find the source of the voice, but it was like it was echoing all around us.

"We told you to stop looking," said the voice. "We told you to stop trying to find Roger, but of course you didn't listen." Suddenly, there was a rustle in the bushes around the perimeter of the field, and two people walked out. I let out a gasp.

"You have just made it harder for yourselves," said Mr. Poli. And at his right side is Roger. Well, not Roger. The Soul Stealer.

"Mr. Poli?" I questioned. "What are you doing here?"

"Well stopping you from making a mistake. I can't have you ruining my plans," he said with a smile on his face. "I'm really not the bad guy, Jeremy. I'm just doing what I have to for a better tomorrow."

"Yeah, and what is your big plan?" Rohan asked. "And how do I fit in?"

"You think I would just tell you my big plan, right off the bat? What if you somehow survive this, and tell the other teachers? But of course, then again, none of them would believe you. I really thought that you would have figured it out by now. But I guess since I'm going to kill you, I can let you in on a little bit of it. Why don't we have a seat?"

Suddenly, my legs started walking without me telling them to. They started moving one foot in front of the other toward Amanda and Rohan. Right as I got to them, it was like an invisible force pushed me down into a sitting position, the wet grass getting all over my pants. The same thing happened to Amanda and Rohan. Mr. Poli started to walk toward us, with the Soul Stealer on his tail. I started to panic.

"Don't you just love magic? It makes life so much easier! You want to have a best friend, but no one likes you? Use psychology to make them like you. You want to start a garden, but are too impatient to watch it grow slowly but surely? Use botany to make it grow quicker. And there are so many more things that we can do! Just imagine how much more we could do, just by having the whole population know about magic, not just the few who are 'good enough' for it? I want to bring magic into the everyday life, and Jeremy, you are the key to it all." I wore a visible face of confusion. What did that mean? I was the key to it all?

"What?" I asked. I tried to look over to Amanda and Rohan to see if they understood, but when I tried to move my neck, I found that I couldn't. "What is that supposed to mean?"

"Have you ever wondered why you look different than everybody else? The blue eyes, the light skin? Well I know why you're like that."

"What?" I questioned again. "How do you know? And what does Rohan have to do with all of this?"

"You were just our first attempt," Mr. Poli said, looking toward Rohan. "Unfortunately, there were some complications when we tried to remove you from the picture. See, all three of you are special. Some," he said looking toward Roger and Amanda, "are bad kinds of special. And some are the good kind," he said looking toward me.

"And what makes us so special?" Rohan asked, questioningly.

"Well let's just say that I know a very powerful someone. I think you both know her," Mr. Poli said looking at Amanda and Rohan. "Her name is

Yvonne." I heard a gasp come from beside me: Amanda. Her eyes were wide in fear and astonishment.

"What is he talking about, Amanda?" I asked.

"Yvonne is the name of my mother," Amanda replied, face scrunched in confusion.

"And let's see," continued Mr. Poli. "Your mother is a tall blonde woman, with a very special mark on her face."

"A mole," Rohan said. I tried to look toward him, confused about how he would know this. "A mole right above her right eye, not much bigger than the size of a pea." Amanda let out another breath.

"How could you know that?" she asked.

"Because that's the description of the person who gave me the bracelet in that church," he replied.

"And remember what she said to you?" Mr. Poli asked.

"That I would need it," Rohan replied slowly.

"And how could somebody possibly know that you would need that exact thing at that exact time? With such confidence? And it actually came true? Who would know such a thing?" Mr. Poli asked, tauntingly, kneeling down to be eye level with us.

"A seer," Amanda replied, slowly.

"A seer!" Mr. Poli exclaimed, clapping his hands, jumping up in excitement. "You've figured it out!"

"But my mother isn't a seer! She is just a normal everyday woman! How can she be a seer?" asked Amanda, angrily.

"It's simple genetics girl," slyly replied Mr. Poli. "She was working with us. She believed in the cause. But then, one day, she just went rogue. After that, *everything* that we had worked for started to fall apart. Your mother," he said, gesturing to Amanda, "foresaw the three of you coming together to try to stop us. Our plan was to take out you, Rohan, so you wouldn't be able to make that machine, but of course our dear friend Yvonne had to get in the way of that. She gave you that bracelet so you would live that day, so you could stop us. But I can assure you, you won't be able to accomplish such feats. I've already moved on from that slight setback. I have figured out another plan. And it involves the three of you."

"We will never help you," I told him, trying to sound brave.

"Well you didn't even give me the chance to tell you what you can do. With you three on our side, we can finally bring magic to the public."

"And how do you suppose we do that?" I asked, a little intrigued.

"Well let's start with Amanda. Since your mother is a seer, and you are studying astrology, I believe that you may have inherited some of her, how do I put it, compatibilities. And with the power of astrology, we can maximize that power, and help you reach your full potential!

"Next we have Rohan," Mr. Poli said, walking to stand in front of him. "Since you are now immortal, you can be our test dummy. Or our human shield, whichever terminology you prefer. If anybody tries to stop us, you can go in and they can't do anything to you, because you can't die. It's brilliant!

"And lastly, Jeremy." Mr. Poli walked in front of me. He looked down at my kneeling body and gave me a smile. "You are the person who is going to make this idea a reality. In order to get you here, I needed a way to bait you out. I figured if we did what we did to Roger, it would work. Obviously it did."

"So you just used Roger to get to me?" I asked, shocked. How could anybody do something like that? "You killed an innocent person just to get to me?"

"Well, technically yes, but for the greater good, I can assure you. With your psychic abilities, combined with mine, as well as the help of the Psyche Tree, we can disperse the knowledge and how-to of magic. Together, we can change the world."

"You're a monster," I told him.

"Well actually he is the monster," Mr. Poli replied sarcastically, motioning to the Soul Stealer. "But also, let's get back to the reason you look different than everybody else. While you have one foot in the human world, you have your other firmly planted in a...different world, shall we say."

"What are you talking about?" I asked.

"Come on, we're so close! Do I seriously have to spoon-feed you this? You, Jeremy, have powers of a god; you, Jeremy, are part divinity."

CHAPTER EIGHTEEN

"WHAT? WHAT IS THAT SUPPOSED TO MEAN?" I ASKED. "HOW IS that even possible?"

"I will let you figure that out on your own," Mr. Poli replied. "But as you see, I now need you three. You three are essential to the next step into the future. I will let you talk it over," he said, turning away from us. Suddenly, I felt as if a giant weight had just lifted off of me. I tried to get on my feet, and found that I could. Amanda and Rohan did the same, and we slowly walked away from them, careful to not turn our backs from Mr. Poli and the Soul Stealer. Once we got out of earshot of them, we formed a little huddle and talked it over.

"We can't trust him," Amanda said first. "I mean, who's to say that he is telling the truth? What if he has a bigger plan, and if we help him, we will just be bringing evil into the world?"

"You're right. But after what he did to Roger, and what he tried to do to you," I said, looking at Rohan, "What's to say he won't do it again? How many more innocent lives is he going to take before we join him?"

"We just have to stop him now while we can," Rohan said. "Come on, they are just a psychologist and a zoologist. We are an astrologist, engineer, and psychologist. We can take them." We were silent for a couple of seconds, and until I said something that had been on my mind ever since we had arrived at Mrs. Hearther's.

"It's just...wouldn't it be nice for people to be able to have access to magic? Think of how much more we could do!"

"And you're absolutely right," replied Amanda, agreeing. "But this isn't the way to do it. Maybe that's how we change the world. Maybe we can train other people in magic, and we can spread it, but not with him. He is going at this all wrong."

"Okay, but what do you think he will do if we refuse? He's probably going to kill us," I reasoned.

"He can't kill me. I'm already dead!" joked Rohan, trying to lighten the seriousness of the situation. I tried to suppress a laugh, but failed to, and even in the seriousness of the moment, let out a giggle. We laughed for a couple of seconds until we regained our composure.

"Just stay close to me, if he does attack, I can try to teleport us out of here," said Amanda, now serious.

"Alright," I replied. We broke from our group, and started to walk back toward Mr. Poli and the Soul Stealer. "We will not join you," I said to him, sticking out my chin. I was expecting a look of shock or sadness on his face, but rather, he let out a little smirk.

"I was hoping you wouldn't say that," he said. He looked over toward the Soul Stealer, and gave it a little nod. The Soul Stealer nodded back, and it turned to face us. It slowly walked toward us, and as it did, he closed his eyes, and raised his arms. As he did that, it was almost as if the entire forest came to life. The branches in the trees started to shake, the birds started calling out, and I could hear a few howls in the distance. He was bringing all of the animals in the forest here!

"Rohan! He's calling to all the animals in the forest. I can't use my mind link on him. Use your scraps to attack him." He nodded his head in recognition, and reached deep into his pocket. He pulled out two long metal screws, and tossed them into the air. Then, with a flick of his finger, he sent both of them flying, straight toward the monster's eyes. The Soul Stealer opened its eyes, right as the screws were mere feet away from his face, and gave us a little smile. Then, right as the screws were about to gouge themselves into its eyes, a black streak flew straight across its face, blocking the screws. The black creature fell to the ground, dead, with two screws stuck in its body. Blood stained the grass around the limp raven. I gasped in horror.

Then, with its arms still raised to the sides of it, a large group of birds landed on the Soul Stealer's arms, one by one, until they were covered with ravens and jays. Even two owls landed on each of its shoulders. Out of the bushes came a pack of wolves, five or six, all looking like they hadn't had a good meal in days. They walked next to the Soul Stealer, and waited there, ready to pounce. Even a couple of squirrels jumped out of the trees, and made their way toward the Soul Stealer. But they all had the same look on their faces: hunger. I started to panic.

"I think we should have listened to you," I whispered to Amanda.

"Oh really? What gave you that idea?" she replied sarcastically.

"Can you teleport us out of here?" I asked back.

"Yeah, just get a little bit closer," she replied. Rohan and I shimmied closer to her, trying not to make Mr. Poli or the Soul Stealer notice. She closed her eyes, and it seemed like she was concentrating very hard to get this right. Suddenly, she let out a blood-curdling scream.

"Oh, and of course since you know our secret, I can't have you teleporting away," said Mr. Poli. "So it is either join us, or die."

"We already told you, we will never join you!" Rohan yelled at him. He pulled back his hands, dislodging the screws from the raven, and brought them back toward us. Right before they hit us, he put his palms out and they stopped. He grabbed them midair, and placed them in his pocket, staining his pants with blood. "Great, now, I'm going to need new pants."

"You won't need pants if you don't have any legs to put them on," said the Soul Stealer and as he did this, he looked down at the wolves, squinting his eyes at them, as if giving them an order. Then, the wolves looked toward the three of us and started charging, slowly at first, then faster and faster, eyes locked on Rohan. I looked over to him and saw fear in his eyes. Then, his eyes narrowed in concentration. He reached into his other pocket, and pulled out a spare piece of metal, one end sharp as a needle. He tossed it into the air.

"What are you going to do, kill these wolves? They didn't do anything to you," I said. "It's the Soul Stealer and Mr. Poli we need to worry about."

"Remember, we already tried that, and it didn't work. We just have to get rid of all of their resources so they don't have anything to use. Then, we can go for them." Just as he finished saying that, the piece of metal came down, and right before it came into contact with his hand, he flicked his hand forward, sending the metal flying toward the wolves. The wolves seemed unfazed by this, and they just kept running at Rohan. I looked away, not wanting to watch what was about to happen. I heard a slice of skin being cut, and then a whimper. I dared to look up and immediately regretted it. The look of anger was gone from the wolves' faces, and was replaced by a look of sadness.

Then, one by one, the wolves all fell to the ground. Rohan had killed them all. I looked toward the Soul Stealer and Mr. Poli, and saw a look of frustration and shock on their faces. I realized that this was my chance. If I could get into Mr. Poli's head, I could end this all now, before anybody else got hurt. I concentrated on Mr. Poli, and did as I had done plenty of times before in his class. I heard a ringing in my head, and looked over to see Mr. Poli wobble, and then hold his head. I let the ringing take over me, and closed my eyes. Once I heard the ringing stop, I opened my eyes. But when I did, I was no longer in the field with Amanda, Rohan, and the Soul Stealer. Instead, I was in a blue fog, kind of like the one I was in when I tried to go into Roger's mind. I looked around to see if I could see anybody like I did last time. Was I in Mr. Poli's head? Did I do something wrong? I looked behind me, and right there, was Mr. Poli.

"Welcome to my mind," he said.

"But I thought I got that under control," I said, confused. "How am I here?"

"You know I don't like repeating myself, Jeremy. As I said, you are in my mind. When you tried to use your mind link on me, I guess it brought you here." I figured that since I was here, I might as well face him.

"Why are you doing this? I mean, if I am being honest with myself, I kind of agree with you. But you are going at this the wrong way."

"There is no right or wrong way. Magic should be for everybody to enjoy!"

"Yes, but as I said, you are going about this the wrong way! You should be working with the people at Mrs. Hearther's to do this. By going rogue, and killing people, they are going to think that you are against them. You have just turned what could be many allies, enemies!"

"No, be quiet!" Mr. Poli screamed, shaking his head. He brought his hands to his head, as if concentrating very hard. "Let me show you what I see," he said, opening his eyes, smiling.

"What is that supposed—" I started to ask. But before I could finish my sentence, I felt a weird sensation in the back of my head. It was kind of like the ringing when we used our mind links, but instead of hurting me, it felt comforting. I happily let it take over, and I closed my eyes. I heard a whirring noise, and when I opened my eyes, we were in the middle of the street. Tall skyscrapers surrounded us on all sides. I stumbled back, surprised at the new environment.

"Where are we?" I asked, looking around in amazement. This place was amazing!

"This is the future that I see," Mr. Poli said, looking around as well, with wonder in his eyes. "Look at this," he said, gesturing to a building a few blocks away. There was a group of people controlling a large piece of metal, bringing it up to the top story of a building. Then, after they brought it to the desired place, another group of people slammed it into place. They were making buildings out of magic! "And look at this," Mr. Poli said, turning me around to face the other side of the road. There was a giant dog park filled with dogs and their owners. They all looked so happy, just them and their dogs. This future was amazing!

"I can see now," I said quietly. This was a wonderful future that I would love to live in. But then I remembered what he did to Roger. What he did to Rohan. I couldn't join him. I turned to him. "But I still won't let you do this. You have done so many bad things to get to this place, and hurt so many people. And how do you know that bringing magic into the world won't bring out bad people? Not everything is going to be this great." He looked down toward me with anger on his face.

"How dare you! I did what I had to do to show those people the true meaning of magic! But, as I said earlier, if you won't join me, then you have to die." And right after he said this, he looked over to the people in the dog park. At first, nothing happened, but then they all started holding their heads, screaming out in pain.

"What are you doing to them?" I asked. He didn't respond. They went on screaming for a couple more seconds, until they finally stopped. Then, they all nodded their heads, and looked toward their dogs. Then, all the dogs looked toward me. And then they started running.

"What did you do?" I asked, frantically.

"Oh, I just commanded the people to tell the dogs to start attacking you," Mr. Poli replied nonchalantly.

"What!" Mr. Poli gave off a maniacal, uncontrollable laugh. The dogs were getting closer, and they weren't stopping. I turned around, and tried to find a place to hide. I started running toward a nearby building that was under construction. A few people were on the sidewalk, and when they saw that I was running toward them, they all stopped what they were doing to form a barricade. I looked behind me and saw that the dogs were still hot on my tail, mouths foaming. I looked in front of me and saw that the people were still there, forming a wall. If I wanted to survive this, I would have to run through them. I braced myself and pushed through the crowd of people.

They held back, but in my fear of being ripped to shreds, I pushed them all away with surprising force. I stumbled through the crowd and finally was let loose. I snuck a peek behind me and saw that the dogs were even closer now. I could now see their black eyes, full of anger. I pushed my feet harder on the pavement, trying to form more of a gap between me and the dogs. I was getting closer and closer to the door of the building. I was a few feet away when I heard a shout from above me. I looked up and saw an elderly lady on an upper level of a building. Her railing was lined with plants. My eyes widened as I realized what she was about to do. Before I could send a signal from my brain to my body, her plants started growing downward at an alarming rate.

Tentacles made of vines, leaves, and flowers shot out toward me. I dodged and weaved the octopus of plants. But a few thorns made their way into my skin, cutting into me. I ducked under a fast approaching vine, and heard a few whimpers from behind me. I looked behind me and saw that the pile of dogs had lessened. The vine had hit some of them. But the ones that were still running were approaching fast. I looked back to the front of me, only to see another vine sweeping toward me. I was too slow to react to it and the vine swept me off of my feet. Somersaulting through the air, I hit the sidewalk with a thud.

Pain coursed throughout my body. I couldn't ignore it now. I slowly opened my eyes and saw that now there was a pack of dogs, a group of people, and dangerous plants all headed toward me. I tried to crawl my way further ahead of me, but I fell to the ground in weakness. I backed up against a wall, fear in my eyes. The dogs were now only a few feet away, with the vines dangling above them and the mob of people not far behind. I held out my hands to protect myself, and let out a hoarse scream. This was how I died.

I closed my eyes, not wanting to see the hungry teeth of the dogs come down on me. I heard them only a few inches away from me, and felt something against my face. I cringed, ready to die, but I didn't. In fact, it didn't even feel like teeth. It felt like sandpaper, and was a little wet. It was like a tongue? I opened my eyes slowly, and what I saw amazed me.

All of the dogs were sitting in a perfect semicircle around me, with the lead dog licking my face. The plants had all retracted back to their original places and the people were all standing behind the dogs, smiling down on me. Did I do that? I looked up toward Mr. Poli in the distance. Even though he was many yards away from me, I could see that he was as shocked as I was. One person stepped forward and reached out her hand. I took it tentatively, and she helped me to my feet. I slowly got up, and the lead dog sat down, sticking its tongue out, panting, as if wanting to be pet. I leaned down to rub it and it immediately flopped down onto the sidewalk, belly up. I rubbed its belly for a few seconds, just in awe of what I had done. I looked up to the other dogs, and they looked like they wanted some love too. I gestured with my hand for them to come over, and as soon as I did that, they got up and came over, almost all in sync. And that was when it hit me.

"Bark three times," I told the dogs. Then in unison, they barked one, two, and three times. "Spin in a circle," I said, growing more excited. They all spun in a circle. The people started clapping. My fear and pain went away in a wash of excitement. I could control the dogs! But how? How could I be a psychologist and a zoologist? And then it hit me like a wave. It must have something to do with what Mr. Poli had said earlier. Because I was part divinity, maybe I can control not just one type of magic. Maybe, I could control them all.

CHAPTER NINETEEN

"W HAT?" SCREAMED MR. POLI, SHOCKED. HE STOMPED OVER TO me, muttering under his breath. "How is that even possible?"

"It's probably because I am part divinity. You have no chance of taking me down now," I told him, looking around at the dogs and humans surrounding me. They all faced Mr. Poli, anger in their eyes for what he made them do. "You are clearly outmatched." He gave me a little smile.

"But you forget, this is my consciousness. I can control whatever happens here." Then, right after he finished saying that, the dogs started to disappear, one by one. The people all turned to me, waved goodbye, and then they too, disappeared. I looked around me in fear as all of the buildings crumbled to the earth, in a mist made of dirt and stone. The ground beneath me started to blink out of existence, until that too disappeared. All that was left was the bright blue sky, surrounding me on all sides. Then, the comfort of the blue darkened until I was left in a terrifying sea of blackness. I floated around aimlessly, not knowing what was up or down. I couldn't even see my hands when they were right in front of my face. I thought I had won, but I forgot that it was his mind.

"Where are you?" I called to the darkness, voice cracking.

"I am everywhere," replied Mr. Poli's voice, coming from all sides of me. His voice reverberated throughout the blackness. Suddenly, it was as if all the air in my lungs started to leave me. I gasped, trying to bring the air back, but that only made it worse. I tried to hold my breath for as long as I could, but that wasn't for long. I could feel myself slipping in and out of consciousness, until finally, I gave in.

I woke up to a feeling of falling, wind pushing against my body. I opened my eyes wide to see that I was no longer in the void, but rather, in the sky. I looked around me, trying to take in my surroundings, but all I could see was the blue of the sky and the white puffy clouds. Soon, I could make out a shape in the distance below me. One square came into view, and then another, and then another. It was a city! And I was falling quicker and quicker toward the pavement.

I started to panic, my breath shortening. But then I remembered what I had learned. I could control other types of magic. I tried to find a piece of metal from the side of one of the buildings, and once one came into view, I focused on it, trying to will it to come to my aid. It started rattling, but it didn't come off of its hinges. I started to grow worried. Then, just as I whizzed past it, the piece of metal flew off, and started coming to me. Once the metal was within arm's reach, I leaned toward it, and grabbed it. I placed it under my feet, and then willed it to fly up, trying to break my fall. I was coming closer to the ground now, and I could make out the faces of people on the streets. They were all looking up at me, but instead of calling for help, or looking worried for me, they all just stared blankly at me, as if they didn't care whether I lived or died.

The ground came closer and closer, and the piece of metal was breaking my fall, but it wasn't going to be enough to fully save me. Then, I thought of the next best idea. I focused on the metal from the buildings all around me, and willed them to come and help me. They all released from the sides of the buildings, making the screws and bolts fly outward toward the people on the ground. But I couldn't worry about them now. They weren't even real.

Once I got all of the metal pieces under my control, I willed them to stack onto each other, with one side touching the ground, and the other up in the air, where I was. Then, right as I was about to hit down, I forced them to bend into an angle, making a slide for me to fall down. I clutched the original metal piece, and prayed for my life. Closing my eyes, I heard the two pieces of metal collide with each other. I squinted open my eyes, and saw that it successfully worked. Sparks flew outward, dissipating in the air. I rode the makeshift slide toward the ground. It was bumpy, but at least it saved me.

Then, as the metal I was riding came to the end of the slide, it shot across the road, and skidded toward the sidewalk. Once it stopped, I leaped out, and took a deep breath, holding my chest, trying to recover. I fell down onto the pavement, off balance from my descent. Unfortunately, I didn't get much time to recover. I was then teleported into another place. This time, a completely black room. I couldn't tell how big it was. The only things in the room were Mr. Poli and me.

"You have to stop this now!" I told him.

"Why? So you can go and stop my plans?" he asked.

"Yes! You are doing this all wrong! You can't just go around hurting people who don't agree with you. Let's say you do go through with this, and for some reason we do help you. The people at Mrs. Hearther's will for sure punish you. And you can't defeat all of the people there. Your plan will never work!"

"Yes! It! Will!" he screamed. Then, I started to experience a weird feeling in my body. Then, my body contorted in different ways it definitely shouldn't. My arms started twisting backwards, making every bone crack and dislocate. My legs cracked and went in different directions. My body was killing myself! But I didn't want to. I didn't want to die. I wouldn't. I let out a scream, louder than any I had before. I broke free of Mr. Poli's grasp, and realized what I have to do.

"You will allow me to leave your mind. You will let us take you in. And you will admit to everything you have done," I commanded him. Mr. Poli started shaking, and his breath became labored, like he was trying to resist. "My magic is stronger than yours," I said, walking closer to him, step after painful step. "You will allow me to leave your mind. You will let us take you in. And you will admit to your crimes," I repeated. The shaking became stronger, but then he let out a gasp, and then fell to the floor.

"Okay," he said sadly. Then he closed his eyes, and I did the same. I felt my head spinning, and I knew that it was all going to be over soon. When the spinning stopped, I opened my eyes again, and I was in the field with the Psyche Tree again. I was lying in the grass, my back wet. Amanda and Rohan were leaning over me, worry in their eyes. When they saw my eyes open, they got excited, and smiled. I tried to stand up, but couldn't, and just lay there.

"What happened?" asked Amanda. "Rohan had killed the wolves, and then you and Mr. Poli just collapsed!"

"I went inside his head," I replied weakly. "I'll tell you about it later." I lay there for a couple of minutes, and once I found the strength to get up, I did slowly, with the help of Amanda and Rohan. I looked over to where Mr. Poli and the Soul Stealer were. The Soul Stealer was lying on the floor, unmoving. Mr. Poli was sitting on the floor, defeat in his eyes.

"Is it...dead?" I asked slowly, pointing to the Soul Stealer.

"No, just unconscious," replied Rohan.

"Good," I replied.

"What are we going to do about them?" Amanda asked, gesturing to the Soul Stealer and Mr. Poli.

"We are going to try to find the real Rohan. And I think the Soul Stealer will be able to help us. And as for Mr. Poli, everything is already taken care of."

"You sure everything is going to be okay?" Amanda asked. "Because last time you said that, it wasn't."

"Relax," I replied. "We won."

CHAPTER TWENTY

"SO DID YOU FIND OUT HOW TO CONTACT ROGER?" ASKED Amanda. Oh no! In my fight with Mr. Poli, I had completely forgotten!

"No," I replied, "But I'll just try what I was going to do before we got interrupted," I said, looking across the field. I slowly walked over toward the tree, and did as I had a couple minutes ago. I placed my hand on the tree, and closed my eyes, thinking about Roger, the real one this time. I could feel the power of the Psyche Tree flowing through me. I thought about Roger, the kind brother who was always looking out for me and Tinna. The brother who cared about everybody and wanted to change the world. I could sense the tree trying to find Roger. Its energy was flowing through the roots, branching out to even the most remote places of Tarenburg. I followed the energy, wondering where it would take me.

The energy went through the forest, and out the way that we came. It shot across the path that we had taken to get here, and to Mrs. Hearther's School of the Sciences. It then went past it to a place where I would have never expected it to go: the void.

Once it reached the void, it started to descend into it. The fog was cleared out of the way for the tree, and in its place was a giant ravine. And it had a bottom! There was a river running through it, and a couple of shrubs, but other than that there was nothing. Yet, the energy just kept going forward. We turned a corner, and I could see a figure lying on the ground. He was shivering, cramped into a corner, with a small fire burning right next to him. He was in a ghostly haze, like he wasn't fully there, but I had never been happier to see anybody in my whole life. It was Roger. A scratched up hazy Roger, but a Roger nonetheless. I went into his head, like I had done plenty of times before. I heard a ringing, and I let it take over me.

"Roger!" I called in my head.

"Huh? What? Who is it?" asked Roger. He jerked up and looked around him frantically. "Where are you?"

"It's me, Jeremy," I replied, trying to comfort him. "I'm in your head! Why are you all misty?"

"Jeremy?" he asked, as if not remembering who I was. Then I felt a wave of relief and happiness flood over him. "Jeremy! This other version of me kicked me down here. I think he took my body and left my soul here."

"That's crazy! We found the fake you. Turns out, it's a creature called a Soul Stealer. It actually all makes sense now. Do you know if there is a way to put the two of you back together?"

"I'm not sure, but I know you can figure it out," he replied confidently. He stopped talking for a couple of seconds, and I let him think over everything. "How are you doing this?" he finally asked.

"I was accepted into Mrs. Hearther's! Just like you!"

"That's great!" he exclaimed. "I didn't know if you would get in or not. So you are studying psychology?"

"Yeah, and we're here to rescue you. How are we going to get through the fog? Last time we tried going down, we couldn't see a thing!"

"Remember, Jeremy," he said, sagely, "There is power in numbers. You have friends right?" he asked.

"I do. One is an engineer named Rohan, and the other an astronomer named Amanda."

"Okay. You will need them. You don't have to do everything by yourself."

"Okay," I replied skeptically. What else could we do to lift the fog? But if Roger said to do it, we should. "Alright, don't worry. We are coming to get you."

"Thank you," replied Roger, grateful. "For everything. I thought I was going to die down here! You were the last person I would have ever thought to come to save me."

"Of course I would save you. I'm your brother. I wouldn't let you die down here." Then, I concentrated on going back to the field with Amanda and Rohan. I felt the energy of the tree leave me. My insides twisted as I was sucked back to the source, the tree. I opened my eyes, and let my hand go off the tree.

"So, did you find him?" asked Rohan.

"I did," I replied. "But first, we have to bring these two in," I said, looking at Mr. Poli and the Soul Stealer.

"How are we going to get them to cooperate?" Rohan asked.

"Mr. Poli shouldn't be a problem. While I was in his head, I forced him to turn himself in and admit to everything he's done. I could also force him to make the Soul Stealer do the same." I walked over to Mr. Poli, and told him to do just that. He sighed, and looked over to the Soul Stealer, who was still unconscious.

"That reminds me," said Amanda. "What happened while you were in his mind?"

"Oh, I almost forgot!" I exclaimed. I smiled, excited to show them what I had learned. "Rohan, give me your screws."

"Why?" he asked, questioningly.

"Just do it," I replied.

"Okay," he said, slowly giving them to me. I grasped them in my hand, blood still on them from earlier. I threw them into the air, and right as they were about to touch down, I flicked my wrist, making them go flying forward. They didn't go very far, and flopped on the ground a few feet away. I then brought back my hand, making them come back to me. They slowly floated back into my hands. I wasn't as powerful as I had been when inside Mr. Poli's head, but I supposed that that was because I wasn't in the real world then. I snatched them out of the air, and then gave them to Rohan. Both Amanda and Rohan looked at the screws, then at each other, then at me, their mouths open.

"But...how...what?" asked Rohan, clearly in shock.

"How is that even possible?" asks Amanda, doing better with her words. "Mrs. Hearther said that once we picked a science, we could only practice that one for the rest of our lives!"

"I think it's because I am part divinity, whatever that means. I think I can control all types of magic. Watch this!" I tried to focus on one of the animals in the forest, and located a squirrel. I told it to come over here, and it listened. The squirrel ran out of the bushes into the clearing, and then stopped for a few seconds. It ran a few more feet, and then stopped. It went like this until it reached me and climbed up onto my shoulder, where it rested.

"That's wild!" Rohan said. But before he could say anything else, there was a groan coming from the direction of Mr. Poli. The Soul Stealer was waking up. Mr. Poli walked over to it, and told it to listen to us. It begrudgingly accepted, and walked over to us, defeat in its eyes. The squirrel jumped down and hurried back into the forest.

"Let's go back," I said. "Do you think you could teleport us out of here?" I asked Amanda.

"I can try," she replied. "Everybody get close to me." We all huddled around her, and she closed her eyes in concentration. There was a rumbling in the sky, and it opened up, revealing a beam of light coming down onto us. It picked us up, and we flew through it, into the stars. It was beautiful up here! I could see everywhere from the main train station, to the lower-class living area, to the Tarenburg Bay, and to Mrs. Hearther's. I saw Amanda searching the land below us, and when she spotted the school, she focused on it, and then another beam of light appeared right in front of the school, and we rode it down. The beam disappeared, and we were left with the school right in front of us. We did it.

CHAPTER TWENTY-ONE

"**M**RS. HEARTHER!" I CALLED THE NEXT MORNING BEFORE breakfast. The night before, we had all gone to our rooms to sleep and commanded Mr. Poli and the Soul Stealer to do the same. We were going to tell her this morning.

"What is it?" she asked, turning around, trying to get to me in the flood of kids going into the dining hall for breakfast. Eventually, after all of them got through, she was able to make her way to us. The only people left in the courtyard were me, Rohan, Amanda, Mr. Poli, and the Soul Stealer. "Well this is an odd group of people," Mrs. Hearther observed. "What are you doing here?"

"There is something very important that you need to know," I replied.

"And it involves these people how?" she asked, questioningly, looking at the mess of a group we were. I would admit, if I was told that there was some important information that I needed to know, and a lower class, middle class, two upper class, and a teacher were the ones to tell me, I would be a little skeptical too.

"Well, actually, I'm not the one who is going to tell you," I replied. I turned to Mr. Poli and gave him a nod. He walked forward and stood in front of Mrs. Hearther, looking her in the eye. This was it. This was the moment where we actually won.

"Mrs. Hearther," Mr. Poli started, "These kids are out of their minds!" What? "They told me to tell you about some conspiracy that I am involved in! They said that Roger here isn't actually Roger, but rather a monster called a Soul Stealer! They attacked me last night!"

"What?" Mrs. Hearther questioned, enraged. "Is this true?" I didn't know what to say. I looked over to Amanda and Rohan, but they were as confused as me. I looked over to Mr. Poli, and saw a little smile creep across his face. I thought my mind link worked!

"I am so sorry that this happened to you two. Especially you, Roger. How could you accuse your brother of such a thing?" she asked, looking toward me.

"But that's the thing! I wouldn't do it to my brother! You think I would want this for him?" I asked.

"Well I don't know why you would do this, but it is punishable with suspension."

"What, why?" asked Amanda.

"Why? Because you attacked a teacher. You accused one of your own as a traitor. That is why!"

"Wait!" I called, but Mrs. Hearther was already turning her back to us. "Pack your bags and leave today. I will call the train for you. Your parents will be informed of what you did."

"But I can prove that what we are saying is true!" I yelled at her. Why wouldn't she listen to us?

"What could you possibly say that will make me change my mind?"

"Because we know where the real Roger is. And we know how to find him," I replied, hoping that that was enough to convince her.

"And where would that be?" she asked, exasperated.

"In the void," I replied, trying to sound confident. Her eyes widened in shock. "This Roger right here isn't the real one. It is the Soul Stealer! He just took the body of Roger to get to me. He said that I was part of his plan. That all three of us were part of his plan," I said, stepping back to be in line with Amanda and Rohan. They nodded their heads, agreeing with me.

"This is preposterous!" Mr. Poli exclaimed. "Do you seriously trust these kids over me?"

"Well now I am interested in what they have to say," Mrs. Hearther replied. "Go on."

"Well, Rohan was their first attempt at stopping us." I explained, "A couple of years ago, Rohan was attacked by the Soul Stealer. It tried to take his life to stop it from meeting us. Show them, Rohan," I said.

"Are you sure?" he asked. I nodded my head, letting him know that it was okay. He picked up his shirt, revealing his giant scar on the front of his chest.

"That is where the Soul Stealer stabbed him," I said, looking up toward Mrs. Hearther. Her eyes widened and she gasped in shock.

"Okay, but that's not enough to prove anything," Mr. Poli said.

"Well hold on," she said. "Why aren't you dead now?"

"That is because of Amanda's mom, Yvonne. Yvonne was working with Mr. Poli and the Soul Stealer. She believed that what they were doing was right, but then she turned against them. She was there when Rohan was stabbed. But before the Soul Stealer was able to get to Rohan, Yvonne gave him a bracelet with an infinity charm on it." Rohan raised his arm, revealing the charm. "For some reason, it gave him the power of immortality."

"I cannot die," he replied, sounding a little proud, but also with some sadness in his voice.

"And the reason Yvonne knew what was going to happen is because she is a seer," I continued.

"She knew that they were going to try to attack Rohan, so she stopped them," Amanda said. "And Mr. Poli believes that some of her seer powers were passed down into me."

"Okay," Mrs. Hearther said slowly. "So let me get this straight. The Soul Stealer was going to kill Rohan so he couldn't join you, but before he could, Yvonne gave him a charm bracelet that gives him immortality and she knew that this was going to happen because she is a seer?"

"Pretty much," I replied.

"Okay," she said. "Do you know how stupid that sounds! I mean, do you seriously think that I would believe that?"

"But you're not done letting me explain," I insisted. "He said that I was the most important part of his plan."

"And why is that?" she asked.

"Well first, ask Mr. Poli what happened while we fought," I replied, wanting to hear his side of the story.

"Well he went into my head, and then attacked me. I tried to stop him, and at first, I was unsuccessful, but after a few minutes, I was able to overtake him and convince him to leave my mind. He said that he would stop, but I guess not," he replied. Now I have him.

"Actually, that's not what happened," I replied, ready to stop them. "You know how I am studying psychology?" I asked Mrs. Hearther.

"Yes," she replied slowly.

"Well watch this," I said. I backed up, and closed my eyes, trying to focus on a nearby animal. I found a fox nearby, just outside the courtyard and commanded it to come to us. Slowly, just like the squirrel, but after a little bit, I heard its footsteps round the corner. It came trotting in, and then sat next to me. "Roll over," I commanded. It promptly rolled over, and I look to Mr. Poli to see a look of shock on his face. Then, I looked at Mrs. Hearther, and saw that she was as shocked and confused as he was.

"And," I started, "Rohan, can I have some metal screws?"

"Sure," he replied, smiling from ear to ear. He reached into his pocket, brought out two new screws, and handed them to me. I threw them into the air, and right as they were about to touch down, I flicked my wrist forward, sending them flying into a tree. I retracted my hand, sending them flying back to my hand. I grabbed them midair, and handed them back to Rohan.

"But...how...what?" asked Mrs. Hearther, flustered.

"While I was in Mr. Poli's mind, I was able to find this new ability of mine. I believe that I can control all of the different types of magic, and you want to know why?" I asked.

"Uh, y-yes please," she replied, still, in shock.

"It is because I am part divinity," I replied. "That's why I look different."

"No!" screamed Mr. Poli. "I thought it was all in my head. I didn't realize that it was all true."

"So you lied to me, Mr. Poli?" Mrs. Hearther asked, turning toward him.

"Well since it is all revealed now, I might as well tell you. Yes it is all real. This isn't Roger. This is a Soul Stealer. We kicked the real one into the void. These three kids were trying to stop us from achieving our goal."

"And what was that goal?" yelled Mrs. Hearther, enraged. By now, some of the other students were filing out of the dining hall, wanting to know what all of the commotion was outside.

"I wanted to bring magic into the world! It doesn't have to be just for the people who you think are worthy! But since you all know my plan now, I guess I can't keep you alive can I?" Then, he closed his eyes, concentrating on us. Then, Mrs. Hearther let out a scream, and her limbs started contorting in different directions, just like what Mr. Poli had done to me. Mr. Poli nodded to the Soul Stealer who closed his eyes also, concentrating on bringing all of the animals here.

"No!" I screamed, and then concentrated on Mr. Poli, trying to get him to stop. Sweat fell down from my face, as my concentration increased. All of the kids had now heard what was going on, and they started filling the perimeter of the courtyard. I kept concentrating, but it was like there was a giant wall separating me from Mr. Poli. I tried to push through it, but it didn't budge. I used all of my power, and kept pushing, and after a lot of concentration, I finally broke through the wall, and commanded Mr. Poli to stop. But it was too late. Right as I did that, Mrs. Hearther fell to the ground, her body limp. Animals from everywhere started coming to the Soul Stealer's aid. Birds of all types flew around the sky, blotting the cheeriness of the sun. I ran to the side of Mrs. Hearther, and went to feel her pulse. She was dead.

CHAPTER TWENTY-TWO

"**N**O!" I SCREAMED, TURNING TO FACE MR. POLI. "YOU KILLED her!" All of the students gasped. Some of them put their hands to their face, trying to hide their tears, while some of them just stood there emotionless.

"I did what I had to do!" Mr. Poli reasoned. "Since none of you agree with me, I guess I will just have to end you, so there will not be anybody to stand in my way! None of you are worthy of practicing magic! I am trying to make the world a better place. Don't you see that?"

"No!" screamed Rohan. "What you are doing is wrong! You can't just go around killing people you don't like!" Then, he took out two screws from his pockets, the same ones I used to demonstrate what I had learned to Mrs. Hearther just a few minutes ago, and handed one to me. He nodded, and I understood him, without the use of a mind link. We simultaneously threw the screws into the air, and then right as they were about to touch down, we flicked our hands forward, sending them shooting, faster than we had ever done before, straight toward Mr. Poli. If you blinked, you would have missed them. There was no way one of the Soul Stealer's animals could have blocked it. The screws embed themselves into Mr. Poli's arms, one on his right, and one on his left. He let out a scream, and looked down in horror at his now bloody arms. He pulled them out one by one, and then threw them onto the ground, staining the tiles with blood.

"I see you don't have the guts to end me. Come on! Do it!" screamed Mr. Poli, arms open wide, exposing his chest. His hair started to come out of place, stray hairs shooting in different directions. His eyes were wide, bloodshot. A giant grin smeared across his face, showing his shining teeth. His suit was now ripped in multiple places. He was going insane.

"We are going to bring you down, but we are going to do it the right way. You are completely outmatched," I said, gesturing toward the group of kids surrounding the courtyard. Most of them looked at me in confusion, not wanting to fight. Some of them already were reaching toward different objects to help them fight. "While we may all be a bunch of kids, there are still only two of you. You can't beat us all."

"Oh, I beg to differ," said Mr. Poli. Then, he looked at the Soul Stealer, and the hundreds of animals still flocking to his side, and gave him a little nod. Then, the animals started charging. But not just at the three of us. They were also headed toward the other kids. Most of them screamed and ran away in fear, but some of them stayed to fight. I looked around trying to see if there were any animals running toward me. As I turned around, I saw two bright red foxes stalking toward me, growling, foaming at the mouth. I tried to think about what type of magic I could use to stop them. I looked around me and saw a few potted plants around. I concentrated on them, trying to get them to come over to me and help. After a few seconds, the roots came up out of the soil, and slunk toward me. The foxes were now getting closer.

Finally, the plant reached my legs and I shot out my hands, trying to make the vines and branches engulf them. They shot forward just like I asked, and right as the foxes were about to pounce on me and rip me to shreds, the plants wrapped themselves around the foxes, pushing them back further. I heard their snarling from inside the plants. They wouldn't hold them for long. I looked around me to see how the other kids were faring.

Some botanists were calling to the plants, and the trees surrounding the courtyard were coming out of the ground, roots flying everywhere. A group of botanists was using those roots to make a pen for the animals, encasing them in there. Then, they closed it off in a giant sphere, trapping some of the animals inside. A group of zoologists was using their mind links to turn the animals around. Most of them were successful, but some of them failed to do so in time, and the animals reached the group of kids. I heard screaming coming from them, and I didn't want to look. I saw giant flashes of light all around me as astrologists either teleported themselves away, or teleported the animals away. The engineers were taking metal parts, and using them to attack the animals.

I heard a rip beside me and looked to the source of the sound. The foxes had broken through the plants, and they looked even angrier now. Leaves and branches were strewn across their feet haphazardly. They ran toward me this time, not wanting to be stopped again. I looked around me, but couldn't find anything to fight with. They were closing in on me, and if I didn't do anything, I would be fox dinner. I did the only logical thing I could think of, and ran. I dodged and weaved through the mass of magic all around me, ducking under branches and jumping over animals. As I ran, I looked to the ground to see if I could find any metal parts I could use, but only picked up a single metal shard, one end at a tip. I kept running, looking behind me every now and then. The foxes were still following me. I ran under the entrance sign and out into the welcome area, where I had first arrived at Mrs. Hearther's a few months ago. There were a lot of kids fighting out here too. Animals were still flooding out of the surrounding forest. Some of them locked eyes with me and started chasing after me, joining the two foxes. I found a tree and tried to make it come out of the ground and fly over to me.

I closed my eyes as I ran, hoping I didn't run into anything. I pictured the tree's roots coming out of the ground, sending dirt flying everywhere. I then imagined it shooting across the field and landing behind me, hindering the animals from following me. I opened my eyes and looked to where the tree was. I smiled, seeing an empty dirt patch where it was. Then, I heard a giant crash from behind me, and the screech of some animals. Dust flew out in every direction and the ground shook beneath me, causing me to stumble and fall. I fell onto the grass, getting a mouthful of dirt.

I spit it out and turned around seeing a turned over tree in the middle of the field. There were no more animals following me. I let out a breath of joy and slowly got to my feet, dusting the dirt off of my pants. I started limping back to the courtyard to see if I could help, holding my throbbing head. I was about to round the corner into the chaos of the courtyard, when I heard an all too familiar snarl from behind me. I slowly turned, hoping I had imagined it. Standing right behind me was one of the original foxes, hair pointed out in every direction, fur mud-stained, teeth ripped out, but one thing stayed the same. Its eyes were still locked on me. I reached into my pocket and fished out the screw. I tossed it toward the fox, sending it straight into its hide. It let out a howl, but it didn't collapse. I started running again, even angrier.

I turned and ran into the courtyard, with the fox hot on my tail. I heard screams coming from the kids. Some of them were now aiming their magic at each other. Mr. Poli was in the middle of it all, controlling some of the kids, like a great puppetmaster, a ringmaster in a circus of chaos. The kids had no control over what was happening to their bodies. I understood their screams, for I had been a victim to the same situation before. If we wanted to end all of this, we would have to stop Mr. Poli, for good this time. But in order to do that, I first needed to get rid of the fox. And I had the perfect idea. I took a sharp right into the dorm rooms and ran up the grand staircase. The fox skidded into the building, ruining the carpet on the floor. I ran up the stairs, using the guardrails to propel me forward. I shot across the hallway until I came to my room.

I reached into my pocket to try and find my key, but found that it wasn't there. It must have fallen out in the midst of the fighting! If I wanted my plan to work, I needed to be in my room. Out of options, and with the fox now up the stairs, I pushed my back against the far wall and ran into my door, trying to break it open. When it didn't work, I tried kicking at the lock, but that also didn't work. The fox was now only a few feet away from me, and one last time, I tried running into the door. I flattened myself against the wall, and ran shoulder first at the door. It broke off of its hinges, flying into my room and slamming onto the ground. I ran inside, hoping the fox would follow me. I heard its claws creep against the hardwood floor. It rounded the corner and stalked into my room. Its mouth almost turned up into a smile, as if happy I was now trapped. But I wasn't. It had fallen right into my trap. There was nowhere it could run. It circled around me and I focused on the farthest and safest place I could think of for it to go: the Psyche Tree. I pictured the giant tree, spiraling to the heavens. I pictured the branches coming inward to form a giant eye. And then I pictured the fox in that field.

Suddenly, a beam of light appeared in the middle of my room, faint at first, but glowing brighter and brighter. It distracted the fox for a couple of seconds, but those precious seconds were all that I needed. I ran behind the fox and as it looked back to me, I kicked it into the light, sending it, hopefully to the Psyche Tree. The light sucked up the fox, and then disappeared, leaving just me in my room.

I took a deep breath, relieved I was actually able to stop the fox. Stumbling toward my bed to sit on it, I opened up the curtains to see the mess in the courtyard. Plants were broken, strewn around the ground. Animals lay limp everywhere and some kids were on the ground, others attending to their needs. But one thing was common throughout the entire courtyard—the old orange and yellow tiles were now stained with blood. And Mr. Poli was in the middle of it all. How could we stop him? Last time I tried forcing him to stop it didn't work. I wouldn't be able to save Roger if we couldn't stop Mr. Poli here and now. I remembered my short conversation with Roger, how he said that I would need the help of my friends to save him. Maybe it didn't just apply to that situation. An idea started to form in my mind as I hobbled downstairs.

I stumbled down the staircase and into the courtyard. I looked around me and tried to find a few certain people. I saw Emily, the girl whom I had practiced magic with the first day at Mrs. Hearther's. She was running away from a screeching cat. I ran over into their path and picked up a nail on the way. I shot it forward and it grazed the side of the cat, causing it to stumble and fall over, letting Emily run away. She looked around trying to find who did that, and I waved my arms in the air, trying to get her attention. Her eyes landed on me, and she came sprinting toward me.

"What's happening?" she asked, panting, eyes wide with panic.

"Mr. Poli is not who we thought he was. He is the person behind all of this. I'll explain it soon. For now, I have a very important job for you."

"What?"

"I need to find every psychologist you can find and tell them to go into that far corner," I said, pointing to the far left corner of the courtyard.

"Why?" she asked.

"You'll see." She ran away, going to find some more psychologists, while I did the same. I tried to find the people in my psychology class. I saw one kid was being chased by a group of ravens, and I commanded them to leave him alone. They flew away, and I ran over to him to tell him the plan. He nodded, fear in his eyes, and ran to the corner, where a group of people was already forming. I ran to help a few more people, until we had amassed a group of about thirty psychologists.

"The person we have to go after is Mr. Poli," I started. "He is the reason all of this is happening. I tried to use my mind link to command him to stop, but I guess he fought through it and was pretending. But I doubt he can stop all of us." I stopped and ducked as something crashed to the ground. Dust flew everywhere and we all coughed, trying to get it out of our lungs. I looked back to the group, and saw doubt on most of their faces. They didn't think that they could do it. "Come on guys! We are all powerful psychologists. You shouldn't let Mr. Poli intimidate you. We can do this! All we have to do is, at the same time, command him to stop all of this for good."

"Okay," said one boy.

"Let's do this," said another boy. Then, one by one, they all started agreeing, until we were all ready. We turned to the middle of all of the madness, where Mr. Poli was standing, smiling and looking around at the chaos he was causing.

"Now!" I screamed. I focused on Mr. Poli. Mr. Poli, the teacher whom I had looked up to, the person who made me want to study psychology in the first place. Mr. Poli, who had the right idea, but the wrong way of going at it. I tried to get into his mind, and with the help of the other psychologists, we were able to break through the imaginary wall with ease. "Stop what you are doing," we commanded. "Stop all of this. Let us bring you in. What you are doing is wrong." I looked up to Mr. Poli, and I saw him bring his hands to his head, screaming out in pain.

"No!" he called. "What I am doing is right! All of you don't see the good in this! You self-righteous—" But he never got to finish his sentence. He fell to the ground, defeat in his eyes, real this time. I could feel it

"Great job," I told the other psychologists. They all looked around, proud of what they had done together. And they should be proud. I knew I was. Now there was just one more thing to do. "Tell the Soul Stealer to stop," I commanded Mr. Poli. "For real this time. And tell him that he is going to help us get Roger back." I looked across the battlefield, and I saw him look up at the Soul Stealer. He tugged on its shirt, and told it to do that. The Soul Stealer looked enraged, but it couldn't go against its master. It released its grasp on all of the animals, letting them disperse back into the wild.

I looked around to see the damage that Mr. Poli and the Soul Stealer brought to the school. There were some animals scattered on the ground, unmoving. The trees and plants were all upturned, and some of the ground was scarred from the astrologists. Blood was everywhere. Some of the kids were lying on the ground, injured, and the other students were helping them get up, and going to fetch the healing supplies. At least nobody was killed. But we weren't done yet. We still had one more thing we had to do. I walked over to Amanda and Rohan, also in the middle of it all. They looked tired, and their clothes were messed up, but at least they were unharmed.

"We did it! And for real this time!" Amanda exclaimed. Rohan let out a sigh, smiled, and let out a little chuckle.

"But we aren't done yet. We still have to save Roger," I said, looking toward the Soul Stealer. "And I think he's going to help us get to him."

CHAPTER TWENTY-THREE

"WE ARE GATHERED HERE TODAY TO CELEBRATE THE MEMORY of Eliza Hearther. She was a wonderful woman, kind, caring, and loving. She always wanted to do everything in her power to make the world a better place, and she lived by that until the day she died. I know most of you don't know who I am. My name is Jerome Bennet. You may call me Jerome. I was very close friends with Mrs. Hearther," Jerome said, stopping to bring a tissue to his eyes, trying to hide his tears. He took his glasses off of his face and placed them on the pedestal, right behind the casket that held Mrs. Hearther's body.

He took a breath and regained his composure. "When we were little kids, Eliza came up to me and told me that she had found magic. That it was the greatest thing ever! Of course, I didn't believe her. I mean, who would? But then she showed me what she had learned." He laughed. "She could control plants! After she showed me that, I figured, why stop there? I asked her if there were any other kinds of magic, and she said that she didn't know, but it was going to be her life goal to figure it out. And look at her now." Jerome looked down the pedestal, and at the casket, giving off a small smile. "She opened a school and brought magic into the world! Of course, she didn't want to do it without me, and made me the vice-principal. She inspired a new generation of practitioners! And she died doing what she loved. And thanks to all of you, her death wasn't in vain," Jerome said, looking around at us.

"Last week, we were faced with a terrible conflict, and you all were able to overcome it, thanks to Mrs. Hearther's teachings. Each and every one of you are powerful and brave for what you did. I would now like to ask that we all take a moment of silence for Eliza. May she still live on in our memories." Jerome put down his sheet of paper, and placed his head down, his body shaking in tears.

I closed my eyes, thinking about Mrs. Hearther. She really was a wonderful person, doing what she loved. The now clean courtyard was filled with the silence of every student attending Mrs. Hearther's School of the Sciences. After I said my prayers, I lifted my head up, and turned to face Amanda on my left, her eyes glossy, trying to hold back tears. I leaned over and saw Rohan on her other side, unmoving, staring into space. Even the Mallery twins were saying their own silent prayers. Mrs. Hearther had changed all of us for the better. She gave us an opportunity to change the world, and to be better people, and we fulfilled that. But we weren't done yet. We still had to get Roger back.

For the past week, Rohan had been making a machine that could fit four people in it. I told them that all three of us needed to go into the void, and at first they were skeptical, but they eventually agreed that if Roger said to do it, then we probably have to. The fourth seat was for Roger himself. I tried to help Rohan make the machine, but I didn't understand most of the mechanics yet. Since this machine was bigger than before, I was going to help control it. Later that evening, the three of us went to Mr. Ringly's engineering room, where we had been building the machine. Because we were making it so much bigger, we had to build it in his classroom, and he was helping us make it.

"Alright," said Amanda, as we walked into the room. "What else is left to be done?"

"Well since the design is pretty much the same as last time, just bigger, all we need to do is attach the seats on, and then we are done," Rohan replied, going to find a few pieces of scrap metal. He came back with eight pieces, four for the backrest, and four for the seat. Using engineering, I helped Rohan move the pieces into place, under the supervision of Mr. Ringly. After we were done with that, Mr. Ringly walked around the machine, nodded, and smiled.

"I couldn't have done it better myself," he said. "So are you guys going to go out tonight?"

"That's what we're planning on doing," I replied.

"Alright. Be safe. And when you get back, we will have the Soul Stealer here ready for you."

"Thank you," I replied. "You have been such a great help."

"No problem," he replied. "Now go get Roger back." I nodded my head, and then with the help of Rohan, picked up the machine. When we lifted it, it was a little wobbly at first, but we got the hang of it, and slowly made our way down the hallway, with a few students every now and then watching us go by. We made it to the courtyard, where some kids were cleaning up from the funeral earlier today.

Without a word, they cleared a path for us to go through. They knew what we were doing. This time around, everybody knew what we are doing, so we didn't have to be sneaky about our movements, which helped us make it to the void a lot easier than last time. Once we reached the void, we slowly lowered the machine to the ground, and rested for a little. I climbed into my seat, the middle one, and Amanda and Rohan climbed into the seats next to me.

"Remember," said Rohan, now able to talk normally. "Just focus on the fans. If they turn off, we are done for. You just need to command them to continue spinning, but not too quickly."

"I know, I know," I replied. "If they spin too quickly, we will shoot straight into the air. They need to spin, but not too quickly for our descent. Then when we go back up, they need to be going extremely fast to be able to bring us back up."

"Right," Rohan replied. "And I will steer it. Are you ready?"

"Ready," Amanda replied.

"Let's do this," I said. I focused on the fans, and after a few seconds, they started to whir, gaining speed by the second until we were fully off the ground. Then, Rohan slowly brought us over the void. I clutched the side of my seat. I didn't want to fall over. Once we were fully over the void, I commanded the fans to keep spinning, but at a lower speed. They did just that, and then we were descending, slowly but surely, into the void once again. The fog crept up on us, and I started to panic. What if this didn't work? What if the fog didn't clear up, and we wouldn't be able to rescue Roger? I tried to put all of those worries into a box in my head, but the box was too small, and suddenly, all of my worries came flying back, but this time, more intense. But I couldn't let it take over me. I had to stay in control of the machine.

The fog crept up toward us, inch by inch, until the bottom of the fog was touching the machine. Soon, the entire machine was submerged into the fog, and just like last time, I couldn't see anything.

"Can you guys see anything?" I asked Amanda and Rohan.

"Not a thing," replied Rohan, glumly. "What about you, Amanda?"

"What are you guys talking about? The fog is clearing up!" she exclaimed, confused.

"No it's not," replied Rohan, also confused.

"Yes it is," she insisted. "And I can see the bottom! It isn't too far down!"

"How can you see through the fog?" Rohan asked.

"It must be because your mother is a seer," I replied. "I guess because seers can see into the future, they have better vision, or something like that. Maybe you can see things others can't. Perhaps some of those traits really did pass down to you. We need you in order to see through the fog! Which way?" I asked.

"Straight down!" Amanda replied happily. "There is nothing in the way." And so I kept going down, slower this time, just in case. After a few seconds, we were completely submerged in the fog.

"Keep going down," Amanda said. "It's actually not that far down. We are almost there!" Then, as if a giant sheet of paper was ripped from right in front of my eyes, the fog disappeared, revealing the rest of the void. And just like Amanda had said, it wasn't that much farther down.

"Woah," said Rohan, looking around. "That's cool." I was in as much awe as he was.

"Try to land right there," I said, pointing to a patch of land in the middle of a giant river. Rohan steered the machine toward the island, and once we were over it, I slowly started to let go of my hold on the fan. We slowly started to descend, until we touched down with a slight bump. We made it.

CHAPTER TWENTY-FOUR

"THIS PLACE IS AMAZING!" I EXCLAIMED, LOOKING UP THE ancient walls of the canyon. "How do you think this happened? I mean, the fog."

"I have no idea," said Rohan, also in awe of it all. "Also, I can't believe that getting through the fog was as simple as having Amanda come with us."

"I know," Amanda replied. "But the strange thing is, I don't really see the fog. Yes, there is kind of a little bit of empty space between here and the top, but for the most part, I can see through it."

"That's so strange," said Rohan. "So, do you remember which way it is to get to Roger?"

"Well, if I remember correctly, and he hasn't moved since last time, he's this way," I said, motioning to the left.

"Well then let's start our journey," replied Amanda.

"We are finally going to bring him home," I said. "And then this entire nightmare will be over." I started walking to the left, and Amanda and Rohan followed close behind me. Mostly, the ground was full of water, a river leading somewhere far away. This was probably how he survived. Most likely, when he fell, he landed in the water. It must be pretty deep then. I stopped for a second, and started to wade into the water, Amanda and Rohan looking at me questioningly.

"What are you doing?" Rohan asked, lightly placing his foot in the cold, slow-moving water. "Is he in the water?"

"No, it's just an experiment," I said, wading into the river. After a few seconds, and about ten feet into the water, the water level had reached up to my waist. And it still went on for what looked like twice the length of our house back in the upper-class district. It probably went a lot deeper. This was definitely how he survived.

"I just wanted to see how deep the water was," I said, slowly walking back toward the safety of the land. "Let's keep going." We continued our trek, and I could spot many different types of plants. Some were growing in little patches in the cracks of the ground, and some of them were entwining themselves up the walls of the canyon, reaching up to the sky. Somehow, the sun's rays were able to reach it from all the way down here. Maybe it was because the fog wasn't really real, but an illusion, so it didn't actually stop the heat from getting down here. The plants were probably what Roger was living off of. I also don't see any animals, aside from a few small fish here and there. At least there was nothing that could kill Roger here.

We walked in silence for about ten minutes, just listening to the sound of the water rushing past and our footsteps on the damp rock.

"How far is it until we get to Roger?" Rohan complained. "My feet are starting to ache."

"I'm not sure," I replied. "When I was at the Psyche Tree, we seemed to be moving extremely quickly. It only took us a couple of seconds to get to Roger."

"Maybe we should try calling out to him?" Amanda said.

"I'm not sure if that is a good idea. For one, we need to keep our energy in case this becomes a multiple day venture. And also, just because we haven't seen anything that can kill us, doesn't mean that there isn't anything."

"Okay," said Amanda, "I'm also getting kind of hungry." I clutched my stomach as it let out a roar of its own. I had been secretly hungry the whole trip, but I didn't want to say anything.

"Me too," I said, stopping. I sat down and relaxed my legs. "We should find something to eat."

"Do you think the plants are okay to eat?" asked Rohan.

"I mean, you can try them," I said. "They're probably what Roger is living off of, so they should be fine." But before I could finish my sentence, Rohan was snatching a loose vine from the wall, ripping it free. Then, without a second thought, he stuffed it in his mouth, chewing quickly, then forced it down with a giant gulp. His face was quenched in disgust, but soon, that look of distaste turned into a look of shock. He grabbed for another leaf, then another and another, and rather than chewing them slowly and forcing them down, he took his time with the leaves, enjoying the flavor.

"What are you doing?" I asked, confused.

"It's really good!" Rohan exclaimed. "It's rejuvenating. I don't know what is in these plants, but no wonder Roger is still alive!" I tentatively reached for a leaf, skeptical about what was in them, and then chewed slowly, then faster, and faster. I reached for another, then another. They were really good! They had a kind of hard exterior, but the inside was juicy and refreshing.

"These are delicious!" I observed. "But we shouldn't eat too many of them. We don't want to get hooked." Rohan stopped his hand from putting another leaf in his mouth and Amanda finished hers.

"You're right," said Rohan, looking at the leaf, and then throwing it into the river, carrying it to who knows where.

"Let's keep going," I said, getting up, starting walking to the left. "It shouldn't be that far away now." We kept walking for about fifteen minutes, when suddenly, we heard a strange banging sound coming from around a corner. We all stopped in our tracks, fear in our eyes.

"What do we do?" whispered Amanda, scared out of her mind. The banging continued.

"We should go in the opposite direction. Are you sure that this is the way to get to Roger?" asked Rohan.

"Positive," I replied. But now that I think of it, this area did look familiar. The shape of the canyon, the amount of plant patches. And then I remembered; this is the place where I saw Roger. I listened closely to the sound of the banging, and realized that it had a sort of rhythmic beating. Bum. Bu-dum. Bum. Bum. Bu-dum. Bum. Bum. Bu-dum. Bum. No natural thing could keep that tempo. I peeked around the corner, and was never happier to see anything in my entire life. I started to run toward the figure, with Amanda and Rohan behind me.

"What are you doing?!" screamed Rohan behind me. "You're going to get yourself killed!" But I didn't listen to him. I ran over to the ghostly figure of my brother. Once I reached him, I spread my arms around him, giving him the biggest hug I had ever given somebody. He jumped, startled, and let out a scream, but I kept my arms around him. By now, Amanda and Rohan had stopped running, understanding the situation. Roger turned his head slowly to face me, and his eyes lit up like the night sky. A giant smile crept across his face.

"You found me," he said, embracing me in a hug. Before I knew what I was doing, I found myself crying in his arms.

"I missed you so much," I told him, in between tears. "They said they kicked you down into the void, and I thought you died."

"It's good to see you too," Roger replied. "Wait, who is 'they.'"

"Mr. Poli and the Soul Stealer. He said that the Soul Stealer kicked you down here. I didn't know if you survived."

"Mr. Poli was behind all of this?" he questioned. "And who is the Soul Stealer?"

"It's a long story," I told him, still crying in his arms. I took a deep breath, took a step back, and looked up at him. "But it's time to take you home now." For the first time, Roger looked behind me to Amanda and Rohan. They both gave him a tentative wave.

"So you must be Rohan and Amanda," Roger said, smiling. "Thank you for what you did."

"Wait. How do you know who we are?" asked Rohan, looking from Roger to Amanda to me. Amanda looked as confused as he was.

"Well Jeremy told me about you two. He said that you, Rohan, are an engineer, and Amanda is an astrologist."

"That's right!" Amanda said. "It's nice to meet you. But if I may ask, why are you all hazy? It's like you aren't a complete person."

"I think before this 'Soul Stealer' kicked me down here, he ripped my soul from my body. I also believe he put his consciousness into my body. Right before it kicked me down here, it was as if I was looking in a mirror."

"So all we have to do is figure out a way to put your soul back into your body," said Rohan, nodding his head. "But what happens to the Soul Stealer after we do that?"

"To be completely honest, I don't know, and I don't care," I replied. "Just as long as we get you back," I said looking back at Roger.

"Speaking of which, how are we going to do that?" Roger asked. "How did you guys even get down here?"

"I built a machine to get us down here," proclaimed Rohan proudly.

"Hey! I helped too!" I said.

"Wait, hold on," Roger said, putting his hands up, "I thought you said you were a psychologist?" He turned to face me, confusion in his eyes.

"I am," I replied. "But I'm also an engineer. And a zoologist. And an astrologist. And a botanist."

"What? But how is that...oh," he said, the look of confusion turning into a look of recognition. "It's probably because, and I know you may not believe me, you are actually part divinity."

"Wait," I said, now the confused one. "You knew that I am part divinity?"

"You did?" he asked, now also confused.

"Yeah. Mr. Poli told me."

"How did he know that, though?"

"We have no idea," said Rohan, shaking his head.

"But more importantly, how long have you known?" I asked.

"Ever since you were born," he replied, guiltily.

"What! And you never thought to tell me?"

"Well, Dad told me not to so..."

"Dad knew about this too? What about Mom?"

"Mom too," he replied, looking down at his feet.

"Do you know how this happened?" I asked him.

"Yes, but I can't say any more. You'll have to ask Dad when you see him. I'm sorry I didn't tell you earlier. I didn't want to anger Dad, or the gods." I wanted to be angry with him, but I knew that I couldn't. It wasn't his fault. At least, I didn't think it was. But when I saw Dad next, I would ask him. For a couple of minutes, we all stayed silent, me mostly thinking about what I had just learned.

"Alright. Let's go back," I finally said. Roger's eyes brightened up like a million stars. He smiled, and I could feel the excitement coming off of him. You wouldn't even have to be a psychologist to feel it. He nodded his head, as happy as a dog that just found out it was going to the park. We turned around and made our way back to the machine, Amanda, Rohan, and I regaling our adventure, from arriving at Mrs. Hearther's, to going into the void for the first time, to the Psyche Tree, to the fight in the courtyard. Roger hung on to every word of it. We reached the machine, and all hopped in, Roger, Amanda, me, and Rohan, from left to right. I concentrated on making the fans move, and after about a minute, they were up and running.

"You ready?" I asked Rohan.

"Ready," he said. I spun the fans faster, propelling us upward, into the fog.

"Steer to the right," said Amanda. "There's a ledge right above us." I felt the machine tilt slightly to the left, as Rohan commanded it to do so. I continued to push the machine upward.

"We're clear," Amanda said. I kept pushing the machine upward, and suddenly, the sheet of fog was lifted away, revealing the mouth of the void.

"Wow," Roger said in awe of everything. "You three make a really good team!" I smiled, agreeing. Rohan and I worked together to land the machine on a safe patch of grass away from the void. With a little crash, we hit dirt, and we all climbed out. I looked over to Roger, who was looking around the landscape, in awe, as if looking at it for the first time. He smiled, and in the darkness, I saw a small tear fall down his cheek. He let off a chuckle. We were back.

CHAPTER TWENTY-FIVE

"I HAVE BEEN DOWN THERE FOR SO LONG, I ALMOST FORGOT WHAT IT was like up here," Roger observed as Rohan and I maneuvered the machine toward the main courtyard. We rounded the corner to see the last few people cleaning up the chairs in the courtyard. As we walked through, they all looked up from whatever they were doing, and started cheering and clapping. Some kids started calling for the other students to come down. Soon, it seemed like the entire school was here in the courtyard, welcoming back Roger. He had a big grin on his face as we set down the machine, and he walked toward some of his friends. I couldn't hear what they are saying, but I made out a few laughs. Mr. Ringly walked out, and rather than going straight to greet Roger, he walked over to the three of us.

"You actually did it," he observed, in awe.

"We did," I said, equally surprised that we managed to get out in one piece.

"Not that I had any doubts," he replied, putting his hand on my shoulder. "The three of you displayed real courage and skill these past few days. Mrs. Hearther's School of the Sciences is lucky to have you." I smiled, remembering Mrs. Hearther. She would be proud of what we did. "Although, if I may ask, why is Roger all hazy and ghostly?"

"We think it is because the Soul Stealer ripped his soul from his body and took his body," said Amanda. "Now all we have to do is figure out a way to bring the two together."

"And do you have any idea of how to do that?" he asked.

"Not a clue," said Rohan. "But if anybody can figure it out, it's Jeremy." I looked down, trying to hide my blushing. Did they really think I was that powerful and smart? Roger started to walk back over to the group of us, and Mr. Ringly greeted him, welcoming him back to Mrs. Hearther's.

"So, what is the first thing you want to do since you are back?" I asked. "Practice magic, eat all the food you want?"

"Right now, I think I just want to take a shower," he replied, laughing a little.

"Alright," I said. "Go to your room, and take a shower, then you can come to the dining hall to eat whatever you want."

"That reminds me," he started. "I don't know where my room key is. I think I lost it when the Soul Stealer took me."

"It's okay," I said, digging into my pocket. I found the replacement key that the school had given me, and tossed it to him. He caught it with both hands. "You can use my room. Top floor, room 16-228."

"Thanks," he said, giving me a smile. Then, he started to slowly walk to the sixteen-year-olds' building. Once he was out of earshot, I told Amanda and Rohan something that had been on my mind for a while now.

"Guys, I have absolutely no idea what to do."

"I'm sure you'll figure it out," Amanda said. "You always do."

"Yeah but what if I don't? I mean, I don't even know where to start!"

"Let's just review what we know and head over to the library," Rohan said, comforting me.

"Alright," I said, trying to sound calm when in reality I was silently freaking out. "So we know that the Soul Stealer somehow separated Roger's soul and body from each other, and then took it. Now he has the body and abilities of Roger. And Roger doesn't have any magic, but he can still feel things and interact with the world."

"Why don't we just ask the Soul Stealer if it can fix Roger?" Rohan put in.

"But how do we know if it will tell us the truth?" I asked.

"If we force Mr. Poli to tell it to, it can't go against its master," said Amanda.

"But what if since it knows that Mr. Poli lost, it will go against him, because the Soul Stealer won't gain anything out of doing it?" I stated. "I mean, it isn't stupid. Let's go to the library to see if we can find anything about this."

"Okay," Rohan replied.

"It's your brother," Amanda said. I started to walk over in the direction of the library, with Amanda and Rohan following behind me.

"Wait, you want to do this now? We haven't slept all night!" exclaimed Rohan.

"We're so close, I can feel it! I can see the finish line, and I don't want to stop to take a break now!" I argued.

"Jeremy, stop!" Amanda yelled. It is so forceful, and loud, it made everybody in the courtyard stop and look at her for a second. Then, they went back to whatever they were doing. I stopped and turned back to look at them, worry in their eyes. "We need to get some sleep. We can take care of this in the morning." I wanted to agree with them, and I did, but I also want to take down Mr. Poli and the Soul Stealer.

"If you want to take them down, you have to be at your prime. Right now, you aren't," Rohan reasoned. I sighed, agreeing with him.

"You're right. I'm sorry. We'll call it a night and come back in the morning."

"Alright. Try to get some sleep," Amanda said.

"I'll try," I replied honestly, walking back to our dorms. Once I reached my new door, I remembered I gave my key to Roger, so I knocked on it, hoping he was out of the shower. He opened the door, towel around his waist and another one drying his hair.

"Hey," he said.

"Hey," I replied. "If you want to, you can stay the night, and get another key tomorrow."

"Thanks!" he said, brightening up. "You know, I forgot how nice it is to take showers." I smiled and fell into bed. Surprisingly, I fell asleep within seconds of hitting the pillow.

The next morning, after breakfast, Amanda, Rohan, and I were excused from our classes to research how to connect Roger's soul back to his body. We made our way to the library, and once we walked through the mammoth front doors, Amanda and Rohan had the same reaction as I had when I first walked in.

"Wow. This place is huge!" exclaimed Amanda.

"Shush!" called one of the zoologists from the front desk. "No yelling in the library."

"Sorry," she whisper-called back.

"I told you this place was huge," I told them, putting my hands on my hips and looking upward toward the large expanse of books in every direction.

"So, do you know where to start?" asks Rohan. "I mean, there are books everywhere."

"We can go to the section where I found the information about the Soul Stealer in the first place," I said, already walking there, with Amanda and Rohan hot on my heels. It took us a good fifteen minutes just to walk to the section because the library was so big. From the outside, it didn't look that big, but when you walked inside, it was almost as if it went on infinitely. I wondered if there was an end to it. When we finally reached the section about emotions, I found the book that I had picked out to learn about the Soul Stealer, and flipped to the page about it.

"Alright," I started. "I'm going to read this part. Why don't you guys see if you can find any other books about the Soul Stealer."

"Okay," they both said, splitting up into both directions. I looked back to the book and started reading it. It was mostly about what the Soul Stealer was, and how it took its hosts. It said that the Soul Stealer had some psychic abilities that allowed it to do so. Just like a regular psychologist, it went into the person's mind, and told it what to do. Then, with its power, it could replicate the body and abilities of that person. But it didn't say how it can replicate it, or how to reverse it. But if I could reverse the process, and use the help of the other psychologists, we might be able to do it. I closed the book and walked over to find Amanda and Rohan. Amanda was hunched over reading a book.

"Did you find anything?" I asked her. She looked up, startled, and I apologized.

"No," she said glumly, putting the book back on the shelf. "What about you?"

"I think I may have found something. I don't know if it will work, because it doesn't specifically say it, but it is the only thing I have found. I'm going to go ask Rohan now."

"Okay," she replied. I walked over to Rohan, who was running his finger down the rows of books, trying to find one.

"I've got nothing," he said sadly looking at me, keeping his finger on the last book he checked.

"I think I have something," I told him. "I don't know if it will work, but we have to give it a shot."

"Alright," he replied, taking his hand off of the book he was holding on to. We walked back over to Amanda, and on our way out, I grabbed my book off of the ground. I went to check it out, and then we were on our way.

"Good luck," said one of the older zoologists. "Please bring him back."

"We will try," I replied.

"So, what is this plan of yours?" asked Rohan.

"Well, it said that the Soul Stealer just goes into the person's mind, and replicates the body and abilities. So I'm thinking that if it just takes that to do it, maybe it just takes a group of psychologists to bring him back."

"Hmm," said Rohan. "It could work."

"I will go get all of the psychologists, and you guys go see if you can find Roger," I said.

"On it," they replied, walking away to try to find him. I walked into the courtyard to see if I could find any of the psychologists out here practicing their magic before class, and sure enough there was a small group of them practicing in the corner. I walked over to them, and told them my plan.

"Do you really think that this will work?" one of them asked.

"Honestly, I have no idea, but it's worth a shot. Gather every psychologist you can find, and tell them to come here. I am going to go get the Soul Stealer." They nodded, running off in every direction, and I started walking to the prison. Well, the makeshift prison. Because there had been no incidents like this before, we didn't have a place to keep monsters, so we set up one in Mr. Poli's now empty office. I cracked the door open, and I was flooded with darkness. I flipped on the light switch, and I was met with the Soul Stealer, tied down to a chair in the middle of the room, with a blindfold across its face.

"Well hello," it said, tauntingly. "Who do I have the pleasure of speaking to today?"

"You're coming with me," I said, in the most intimidating voice that I could muster. Sadly, it came out as a little squeak. Even with the mask on, the sight and thought of the Soul Stealer and what he did still terrified me.

"Ah, the boy," he said coldly. "Jeremy was it? And why do you need me?"

"That is none of your concern," I told it. I walked over to the Soul Stealer and ripped the covering from its head, revealing the face of my brother. "And don't even think about escaping. We stopped you once and we can do it again."

"Do you seriously believe that you, a mortal human, can hurt me, one of the most powerful creatures in existence?"

"I am even more powerful than you can ever imagine. So either come with us willingly, or make us bring you," I said, leaning against the far wall, farthest from him. I cross my arms around me, still trying to seem intimidating. The Soul Stealer opened its mouth, then closed it again, as if it was going to say something, then decided against it. Then, it said something I didn't imagine it would.

"Ah, whatever. Let's do this," it said, trying to stand up out of the chair, before remembering its arms and legs were still tied up. I tried to suppress my shock, but I sensed some came through.

"Just like that?" I asked. "No demands, or arguing?"

"Well let's just say that this somehow actually works," it started. "Which I doubt it will, my consciousness will just be released from this body and I will go back to where I came from. Another master will seek me out and I will be back. There is no stopping us." I slowly walked over to it, knife in hand, suspicious of its intentions. I stopped right before getting to it and took back my hand.

"What? I know defeat when I see it. Mr. Poli has been defeated, there is no denying it. Plus, even if he wanted me to join him again, he didn't keep up his end of the deal. I have nothing to gain from working with him anymore, so there is no need to continue with him." For some reason, I believed it, even though I didn't want to, and before I could convince myself otherwise, I let it go, cutting the ties that bound it down. It slowly stood up, and rubbed its wrists, sore from a week in chains. I kept my hold on the knife and with it, motioned it to walk out the door. It put his hand up, and gave me a little smile before exiting the dark room of its torture. It squinted its eyes shut as it saw the light for the first time in a week and brought its hands to cover them.

"To the courtyard," I commanded, pushing it along. We walked there, slowly but surely. We rounded the corner of the building and walked out into the sunlight of the courtyard. A look of shock crossed my face for a second as

I saw the people who were in it. It looked like everybody in the school, in-cluding the teachers, were lined up against the wall, waiting to see what would happen. In the middle of the courtyard was the same group of psychologists from when we defeated Mr. Poli, as well as a few more. Amanda and Rohan were also standing in the middle, right next to the ghostly soul of Roger. Roger looked up at the Soul Stealer and shock could be seen across his face, and then tears.

"Are you ready?" I asked him, walking over to the group.

"I think so. Is that really it? The Soul Stealer?"

"It is," I replied, looking back at it. It gave Roger a little smile and a wave.

"We're ready to put you back together though," I said reassuringly. "And I don't think the Soul Stealer will be a problem." He nodded his head, and I turned away to face the Soul Stealer. "Stand right here," I said, pointing to a spot right in front of Roger. It walked there, eyes on Roger the entire time.

"And so we meet again," it said, chuckling maniacally.

"Let's just get this over with," Roger said, sighing. I walked over to the group of psychologists, and told them my plan.

"I know that you have been right before, but we have never faced a mon-ster before," said one kid.

"Yeah, how do you know that doing this isn't going to eat us up or some-thing?" asked another.

"We just have to have faith that it doesn't," I replied, truthfully. "Just con-centrate on the Soul Stealer's body, then on Roger's soul, and just will them to connect, leaving Roger as one and the Soul Stealer as, well, whatever it is."

"Okay. Let's do this," said one, then another, then another, until they were all in on it.

"For Roger," said Emily.

"For Roger," I repeated. Then, I turned to face the Soul Stealer and Roger, and so did the others, forming a circle surrounding them. Amanda and Rohan retreated to the walls of the courtyard. I closed my eyes and concen-trated on the Soul Stealer. The pure evil monster that it was. The one who took over my brother's body, just to get to me. I felt a tingling sensation in the back of my head. It was working. I moved on to Roger, the kind, loving brother who always wanted to help others, and would be friends with anybody. The ringing got louder and louder until it was all that I could hear. I kept concentrating on them, and thought about Roger's body and soul, and making them come together as one. The ringing continued, but I could see a bright light seeping through my eyelids. It was working! I kept concentrating, and the ringing filled my entire body. Then, I heard a voice break through the ringing, telling me something. It was the voice of the Soul Stealer, not of my brother, but a raspy, yet somehow shrieking voice. I wasn't sure how I knew that it was the Soul Stealer, but I did.

"Remember what I said," it told me in its hoarse voice of a thousand souls. "Another master will seek me out and I will be back. There is no stopping us." Then the voice started to get softer and softer, as did the ringing. I opened my eyes and saw the courtyard flooded in light. It was like there was a second sun in the middle of the school. The Soul Stealer looked over to me, and gave me a wink, before looking up to the sky. Then, darkness seemed to pour out of its eyes and mouth, twisting its way into the wind. I heard gasps coming from the outer edge of people in the courtyard. The psychologists were now all staring up at the Soul Stealer, looking at what they had just done. After a couple of seconds, the darkness dissipated into the air.

Then, out of the corner of my eye, I saw something disappearing: Roger's soul. He looked down at his hands, and saw them disappearing as well. Then, he looked up at me, and gave me a little smile. Rather than the darkness of the Soul Stealer, when he disappeared, a blue and yellow light started to come out of him, and was released into the sky. Then, once all of Roger's soul had been transformed into a blue and yellow light, the same process happened when we removed the Soul Stealer, except in reverse. The light seeped into the body's eyes and mouth, until all of it had been consumed. Then, the body opened its eyes, and gave off a huge ear-to-ear smile.

"I'm back," he whispered. I smiled back at him, and reached out to give him a giant hug. "I'm back!" he called out louder this time, and the entire school, students and teachers alike started celebrating, clapping, whistling, and cheering. I looked over to Amanda and Rohan and saw them cheering as well.

"Thank you," I mouthed to them, in between smiles. They nodded their heads in understanding, and continued cheering and clapping. We had actually done it. We saved him.

EPILOGUE: GRADUATION DAY

TODAY WAS THE DAY. AFTER MANY MONTHS OF TRAINING, THE DAY was finally here: graduation day. Today we could finally graduate from our first year at Mrs. Hearther's School of the Sciences. But I wasn't just excited because it was graduation day. My family was coming too. And I could finally face my father.

"Are you ready?" asked Rohan, picking the last pieces of dandruff off of his shirt. For graduation, we were required to wear a formal shirt given to us that represented which magic we were studying. I had to wear a baby blue collared shirt with an eye symbol embroidered in the top left corner. Rohan's was a light red with a wrench on it. Amanda's was a bright sunflower yellow with a star in the corner. The botanists were a leafy green with a sapling in the corner. And lastly, the zoologists were a dark black of the night sky and had a chicken in the corner.

"I think so," I replied, also checking for any dust on mine. I picked the last piece of dust off of the middle of the eye and turned around to face Rohan. "How do I look?"

"Spotless," he observed. "Let's go check on Amanda."

"Okay," I said, looking at myself one more time in the mirror. We walked out of Rohan's room and crossed the hallway to Amanda's room. We knocked our special code, and almost immediately, the door was opened revealing Amanda ready as well.

"Well don't you guys look dapper," she said in a sarcastic voice.

"Ha ha," I said back, equally sarcastically. "You look good too," I observed.

"Thanks," she replied. "Are you guys ready?"

"We were just about to ask you the same thing," said Rohan.

"Alright then. Let's go," Amanda said, closing the light in her room and walking out into the hallway with us. The three of us walked side by side, excited for the day ahead of us. We walked into the courtyard and saw a couple of people milling about, some staying in the courtyard talking to their friends, and some walking into the dining hall. For the ceremony, the dining hall had been converted into an auditorium. The rows of tables had been replaced with seats where our family would be sitting. A stage had been erected on the far end, with five groups of chairs and a podium in the middle. We all parted ways, Amanda going to the group of chairs in the front right with the rest of the astrologists, Rohan going with the engineers in the back left, and I went to the middle section of seats, which were designated for the psychologists. But before I went to my seat, I noticed the zoologists were right next to me, and sitting at the very end was Roger, talking up an excited storm with his friends.

"Hey," I said, interrupting his conversation. He turned to face me, and his face brightened up.

"Hey Jeremy!" he exclaimed, getting up to give me a giant hug. "Are you ready?"

"I am," I said proudly. "How about you?"

"I think so," he said, excitedly. But then, his face got pouty and he didn't look as happy any more. "This next year will be my last year at Mrs. Hearther's. I mean, yes I will be helping the world, but all of the friends I have made, all of the amazing people here, I won't be with them anymore." I tried to comfort him the best that I could.

"It's okay," I said. "Let's just celebrate today, alright? We'll worry about that later. And just think, when you are out helping the world, you will meet all new people and become friends with even more. And I'm sure they won't send you out on your own. You'll still be with some of your friends. I'm sure of it."

"You're right," he said, nodding. "I'm sorry."

"It's okay," I replied, going back to my seat. Every section had four rows, the front one for the sixteen-year-olds, the second row for the seventeen-year-olds, and so on. I took my seat in the front row, right next to Emily.

"Are you excited?" I asked her. Although I could already tell from the beaming smile on her face and the way her knee was shaking that she was even more excited than I was and couldn't wait.

"You don't even know," she replied, her smile getting bigger. "What about you?"

"I am," I replied. But then, a group of people walked in who changed my entire mood. It wasn't that I was afraid to see them, it was just that I hadn't seen them in what seemed like forever. I almost forgot what they looked like. The man was wearing his usual black pastor robes, and he had a blank, nonchalant face. The woman had her glasses perched up on her nose, and like usual, was carrying a stack of books. Just like the man, her face was unreadable. Then there was the little girl, hopping around, unable to control herself. She scanned the group of people in front of her, and when her eyes met mine, her eyes somehow glowed even more than they already were.

"Jeremy!" Tinna screamed, trying to run over to me, but Mom held her back. Both Mom and Dad looked up to where Tinna was pointing, and when they saw me, gave me a small nod, without a smile.

"Your family?" Emily asked, turning in to face me.

"Yep," I replied, looking over to find Roger to tell them that they were here, but when I looked toward him, he was already looking at them. I was a little glum, as I had never gone with Mom and Dad to one of Roger's graduations, and now they were letting Tinna go with them. But I supposed that I had always been in the house to look over her while they were gone, and now since there was nobody else there, and my parents hadn't thought about getting a proper babysitter, they had no choice but to bring her. I wanted to run up to them and explain everything, but I had to wait until the ceremony was over. I looked over at Tinna, a small ball of enthusiasm. It seemed that all she wanted to do was escape Mom's grasp and run over and give me the biggest hug in the world. I wasn't sure if she would be able to contain herself until after the ceremony. I guess we would just have to wait and see.

We waited for a couple more minutes as the late kids and parents started to file in. Once everybody was seated, Jerome walked onto the stage, hushing the audience and students.

"Hello everybody!" he called in a booming voice. "And welcome to graduation day!" The audience let out a cheer, and I looked over to my family, hoping to see them at least clap a little, but Mom and Dad were just sitting there staring at me, while Tinna jumped up out of her seat and started screaming with the other families. After everybody got quiet, Jerome started talking again. "Most of you probably don't know who I am. My name is Jerome Bennet. Up until this year, I was the vice-principal of Mrs. Hearther's School of the Sciences. Most of you who are regulars and have been to one of our graduations before would know that Mrs. Hearther herself would be giving the speeches. Sadly, she will not be able to make any more." Jerome stopped for a second, wiping a single tear from his face. "Eliza Hearther, earlier this year, was murdered by one of our own." An audible gasp came from the audience. Some of them started whispering frantically toward each other. Mom and Dad looked toward each other, and fear crossed their eyes for a split second, before going back to the stone-faced parents they were.

Once the audience stopped whispering, Jerome started talking again. "Thankfully, we were able to find the person who killed her, and he will face the consequences of his actions. This terrible, dastardly person was none other than our esteemed Mr. Poli. For those of you who don't know, Mr. Poli was our first-year psychology instructor. He wanted to release magic into the real world and he killed anybody who stood in our way. Mrs. Hearther was one of those people. He also summoned a monster called a Soul Stealer, which attacked one of our own students, ripped his soul from his body, kicked it down the void, and infiltrated our school, masquerading inside the body of the student. This student's name is Roger Tursoil."

Another wave of shock coursed through the audience, and this time, my entire family had a reaction. Their eyes widened, and Mom opened her mouth, about to say something, but then closed it. Dad just looked angry and Tinna started to cry. Mom tried to calm her down, but failed.

"But don't worry," said Jerome, smiling. "We were able to get him back to his normal and working self, thanks to three special individuals." My family all picked their heads up. I looked over to Roger who started waving toward them. I guess they hadn't noticed him when they walked in. Once their eyes landed on him, a whole new flood of tears came on, but these ones were tears of happiness. Jerome continued. "Now, I am going to announce the names of these three people. All of them displayed real courage and showed what it means to be a part of Mrs. Hearther's School of the Sciences. As I call your names, please stand up. First, we have a first-year engineer. He single handedly created a flying machine to go into the void to rescue Roger. This immortal kid was the first attempt at infiltrating the school, as the Soul Stealer tried to kill him once as well, but failed. Rohan, please stand up."

I looked over to try to find Rohan, and I saw him smiling, getting ready to stand up. All of his engineering friends started to cheer him on as he stood up. Once he was fully up, he gave the audience a wave and they all started clapping again. I looked over to find my family and saw that they were smiling as well, wiping away tears. Tinna was cheering like crazy, jumping up and down, screaming at the top of her lungs. Mom had to calm her down.

"The second person that helped to save Roger is another first-year student. With the power of astronomy, she was the one to figure out that it was the Soul Stealer in the first place. Also, because her mother is a seer, and combined with the power of astronomy, she was able to see through the fog of the void and realized that it wasn't a bottomless pit, but rather a canyon stretching for miles in every direction. This student's name is Amanda."

I looked over to Amanda and she had the same reaction as Rohan. The audience cheered just as loud, if not louder. Tinna went out of control again.

"And last, but certainly not least, this first-year boy studying psychology was the first person to figure out that something was off about Roger. While trying to locate Roger, he created a new sub-form of psychology. While locked in battle with Mr. Poli, this boy was able to figure out that he has abilities that no other person has. He figured out that he can control not one, not two, not three or four, but all five types of magic! This is because he is part divinity! I introduce the third member of their team, Roger's brother himself, Jeremy Tursoil!" I couldn't help but smile from ear to ear, and I forgot that I needed to stand up.

"That's you, silly," Emily said leaning over, reminding me.

"Right," I said, and stood up, giving the audience a wave. A cheer erupted louder than the other two combined. I was surprised that all of Tarenburg wasn't coming to check up on what was going on. I looked at my family and saw their eyes were wide. Suddenly, a waterfall of tears streamed down Mom's face and she had to sit down before she fell over. Dad stood there, eyes wide, mouth agape, and after a few seconds, regained his composure, and gave me a wide smile. Then, he started clapping along with everybody else, and even gave off one whoop. This was the first time either of them showed any emotion besides on Friday nights. Tinna still couldn't control herself and Mom and Dad didn't even try to stop her. I stood there, the cheering washing over me like a wave. I soaked it all in, just standing there looking around the audience. I found Amanda and Rohan and gave them both big smiles. They smiled back. The cheering died down, and everybody sat back down, including Amanda, Rohan, and I.

"Now, let's get on with the ceremony," said Jerome.

After the ceremony, I walked over to my parents, ready to face them. As I walked over to them, it was as if time stopped entirely. Their faces went from irritated, to happiness, and back in the matter of seconds. But it didn't matter what they thought. We saved the school, there was no denying that. Surely they would see what I did and permit me to come back for the next three years. Plus, I also now knew that I was part divinity.

"Hello Mom. Dad. Tinna," I said, as I approached them.

"Jeremy!" Tinna screamed, running into my arms, embracing me in a hug and spinning me around. "I missed you! But I was okay! Because I'm a big girl now! I even put myself to sleep!" she exclaimed proudly, taking her arms away from the hug and putting them on her hips, demonstrating just how much of a big girl she was.

"I'm sorry I was gone for so long," I replied. "And good job on putting yourself to sleep." Once I was done talking to Tinna, I turned to face Mom and Dad.

"So, you really saved Roger?" asked Mom.

"Yes, I did," I said slowly, trying to pick the right words. "But you have to understand, I—" But before I could finish my sentence, Mom reached over and wrapped her arms around me, engulfing me in a ginormous hug. I embraced her back. "I thought that you would be mad at me. I went against what you said and came to Mrs. Hearther's."

"Well, at first we were mad. We were actually very upset with you for most of the year. We almost called the school to take you back," said Dad. "But after a lot of thinking, we realized that it had been your destiny all along."

"What do you mean it was my destiny?" I asked, curious.

"Well since you are half divinity, magic is in your blood. It was only a matter of time," said Mom.

"But for my whole life, you have known. How did this happen? Why didn't you tell me?"

"That's a story for another day," Mom said, reassuring me. I wanted to know now, but I figured that they would eventually tell me. I also wanted to be angry with them, but I knew that I couldn't. It was like what Roger said. They were sworn to secrecy. I was about to let the topic go, but then I remembered one key question that had been on my mind, even before I had left to come to Mrs. Hearther's.

"Dad?" I asked, looking at him.

"Yes?" he asked. I figured I should just get to the point of the question, no going around it.

"Are you an astronomer?" I asked. Then suddenly, both Mom's and Dad's eyes widened in shock, then went back to normal. Dad sighed.

"We shouldn't tell him," Mom said hurriedly.

"He is ready," Dad assured her, looking at me.

"What am I not ready for?" I asked, confused. What did they mean?

"The short answer is, yes. Yes, I am an astrologist," Dad started. I was about to cut him off, but he raised his hand and I closed my mouth. "When I was a little boy, a girl approached me. We had gone to the same early education school. We weren't friends, but it wasn't like we didn't know each other either. She told me that magic was real, and that she could show me. At the time, I didn't believe her, but she kept promising that she could show me. I let up and we went around to the back of the school. She found a sapling in the ground and told us to stop. We sat down right beside the sapling, and she made it grow! It was then that I believed her. That girl's name was Eliza Hearther."

"So you knew Mrs. Hearther, even before she opened the school?" I asked, dumbfounded.

"Yes," he replied. "And so together, with the help of another boy named Jerome, now your principal, we helped to find the different types of magic, and we formed the school, of course, Mrs. Hearther getting the credit for it, as she was the one who discovered it."

"So why didn't you join the school and teach astronomy?" I asked.

"Mrs. Hearther's School of the Sciences wasn't the path that I wanted to go down. When I discovered that I could practice astronomy, it strengthened my belief in a higher being. That is why I joined the Church."

"Oh," I said, finally understanding. "But what about all of those sudden meetings, all of those absences in our lives?"

"Every now and then, some things came up with the school that Eliza needed my help with. For some time now, we had been sensing something wrong that was going on. We had never been able to figure it out until now, with you guys. So I thank you for that. You guys are like some keepers of magic or something. Because of you, magic can stay protected, and there aren't any more threats to the world."

"Okay," I replied, through gritted teeth. I even gave a fake smile, trying to make it as convincing as possible. I still remembered what the Soul Stealer told me that day we vanquished it. Another master would seek me out. There was no stopping us. Who was us? And what was their end goal?